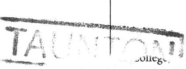

...ə of law to write and publish *At Your Own Convenience: A Guide to Oxford's Loos*. He qualified as a solicitor but never practised, and became a self-employed businessman and ...tr...neur, while continuing creative writing. His children's ...or *Jack and the Monster*, written for and about his middle ...ɔn, was first published by Andersen Press in 1988 and achieved ...nternational recognition in many foreign editions from Japanese ...ʃ: it was even translated into American, where 'Mum'

...'Mom'. Richard has long been fascinated by ancient ..., and has had an interest in archaeology since working as a

...eer on the Masada excavation in Israel during his gap year. ...ised the outline of the story *Knight for a Day* twenty years ...and about his eldest son, Henry, who wanted to know ...would have been like to live in the time of King Arthur. ...Camelot really the last outpost of civilisation amidst the ...esolation of post-Roman Britain, and why is its legend ...h an inspiration? *Knight for a Day* reveals the warfare,

...s and wizardry through modern eyes, providing credible ...s to unsolved mysteries that have been a source of ...tion for centuries.

...LN SELIGMAN also won a modern languages scholarship ...ford and read law. He worked as a shipping lawyer for eight ...before jumping ship to become an artist. He designs large- ...e suspended atrium sculptures for buildings around the ...ɔrld. He also has regular exhibitions of his paintings in London ...nd New York. His set designs for ballet were to be seen recently at Sadler's Wells and Covent Garden. He has illustrated many books a...   ...ا.

and journals in several countries. He lives in London.

Richard Graham

illustrations by Lincoln Seligman

Sagesse Press
LONDON

Published in 2015 by Sagesse Press
28 Hereford Road
London
W2 5AJ

ISBN 978-0-9926301-0-2

Typeset in Maiola by Dexter Haven Associates Ltd, London
Printed and bound in India by Thomson Press India Ltd

Contents

for Henry

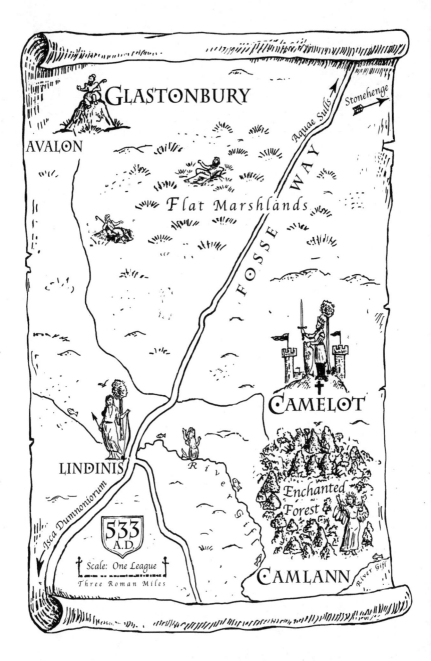

GLASTONBURY

AVALON

Stonehenge

Aquae Sulis

FOSSE WAY

Flat Marshlands

CAMELOT

LINDINIS

River Gift

Enchanted Forest

Isca Dumnoniorum

533 A.D.

Scale: One League
Three Roman Miles

CAMLANN

River Gift

1   The Stone

The stone's primeval magic transcended mortal existence, and only a few very gifted people could sense its super-natural power.

For two millennia before recorded history it stood as a sacred altar at the centre of a megalithic circle and was the focal point for arcane ceremonies. Then the Romans conquered Britain, outlawed the ancient druid religion and moved the stone to an underground temple for the mystery cult of Mithras, where it was used for ritual animal sacrifices. Three centuries later a church was built in place of the pagan shrine and the bloodstained relic was dumped outside in the churchyard.

There it lay unnoticed for several generations until the great wizard Merlin found it and discovered how to direct its eternal energy.

Chaos and disorder reigned throughout the land after King Uther Pendragon was killed without a recognised successor; it wasn't known that he'd entrusted his infant son to Merlin's care. The wizard appointed foster parents to bring up the young prince in secret, supervised his education and hatched a cunning plan to install him on the throne when grown. He embedded a sword in an anvil upon the magic stone with a prophetic inscription:

'Whoso pulleth out this sword of this stone and anvil is rightwise King born of all England.'

For fifteen years the strongest knights and nobles tried to claim the vacant crown by pulling out the sword. However no one could shift it until a young squire called Arthur drew it out with ease, although he was unaware of its significance. Then Merlin showed up and proved that Arthur was the late King Uther's trueborn son and rightful heir, the sole surviving scion of the royal line.

So it was that Arthur became king and brought order and prosperity to the realm. He established a golden age of peace and justice, forming an illustrious fellowship of chivalry and honour: the Knights of the Round Table.

Merlin hid the stone inside a woodcutter's hut in a fairy glade deep within the enchanted forest south of Camelot. This was an otherworldly place, where spirits and dreams could on occasions reveal the patterns of life that shape destiny.

Twenty-five glorious years after, in 533 AD, evil forces invaded the kingdom and threatened to destroy all King Arthur's magnificent achievements.

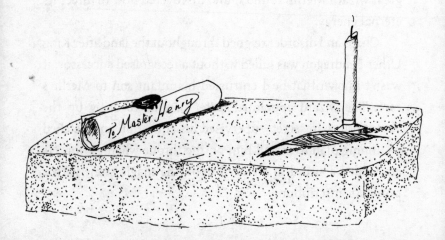

Merlin consulted the auguries and looked into the future. He was now old and frail, but knew he must attempt a risky experiment to avert doom and devastation. Therefore, at the witching hour of an auspicious midsummer night, he focused all his occult powers once again upon the magical stone.

By the ghostly light of a flickering candle he wrote with a scratchy quill pen on a sheet of parchment, checked through his composition and signed it with a flourish. He stuck two objects onto the page, rolled it around them into a scroll and sealed it securely with hot wax. He used his gold signet ring to impress the outline of a fire-breathing dragon into the seal, inscribed 'To Master Henry' on this package and placed it on top of the stone.

The wizard contemplated his handiwork in silence, raised up his magic staff in a ceremonial manner and proclaimed with surprising force and vigour:

'I direct the stone to transport this page
To the boy whom I've seen in a future age.
Convey my summons, candle and potion
So magical powers can set in motion
A journey through time back to Camelot past,
As was foretold when the runes were cast.'

Merlin blew out the flame and struck the stone with three resonating thuds.

The scroll vanished into thin air, and he allowed himself a faint smile of satisfaction because his fateful spell was in progress.

But then an involuntary shiver of foreboding ran down his spine, a chilling reminder about the unpredictable consequences of meddling with the continuum of space and time.

2   The Scroll

Insistent barking punctuates the dawn chorus outside my bedroom window. Today is my eleventh birthday, so I'm far too excited to go back to sleep though I don't feel any different from being only ten. I pull on my tracksuit and tiptoe downstairs to check out what's bugging Jasper, taking care to avoid the creaking step that could wake my family.

To my disappointment my quiet humming of 'Happy birthday to me' hasn't caused any presents or cards to materialise on the doormat; but then our white Jack Russell terrier bounds in through the dog flap and drops a bone at my feet with an enthusiastic wag of his tail.

While hugging my four-legged best friend to thank him for his very doggy gift, I look more closely and see that it's not a dirty old bone at all: it's a rolled-up scroll with 'To Master Henry' written on it in black ink. That's my name, so it must be meant for me, but where could Jasper have found it?

There's no address, no postcode and no stamp, but instead it has a red wax seal impressed with the shape of a fire-breathing dragon. I prise it open and unroll a sheet of parchment that looks like a historical document.

In old-fashioned script there's a poem entitled 'A summons to Henry'. The flowery signature at the foot of the page says 'Merlin'.

A summons to Henry

If you are brave and pure in heart,
Then let a great adventure start.
First bake a cake with special flour,
That has my powdered potion's power.
Two days after the Ides of June,
Precisely five hours after noon,
Go to King Arthur's magic stone
In the fairy glade where you are known,
And bring such gifts as you can handle.
On cake and stone light up my candle,
Walk around it backwards thrice,
And on each circuit utter twice,
'I summon Merlin's magic powers
To take me back to Camelot's towers.'
Swallow some cake, blow out the flame
And seven times call out my name.

Merlin

I like the sound of this magic and an adventure, not least because it refers to King Arthur, Camelot and Merlin. It's the most awesome birthday card ever.

There are two objects inside the package: a candle and a leather pouch, secured by a thong and containing some powder with a spicy smell that I don't recognise.

I read the intriguing summons to 'a great adventure' several times, memorise its instructions by heart and lock it in my desk. The candle and pouch go in my pocket.

Someone must have gone to a lot of trouble to produce the antiquated parchment and imposing wax seal, compose the verse and get it delivered by Jasper at dawn. But who? It's too imaginative for my parents, and my brothers aren't old enough: Jack is nine and George is only six.

I google 'the Ides of June' and solve the first brainteaser: it was 13 June in the Roman calendar. So 'two days after the Ides of June' is today, my birthday. The poem mentions 'King Arthur's magic stone', and that's my secret name for the block of sandstone half-buried in my den: a clearing hidden by trees and bushes at the end of our garden. I imagine it is where fairies would live if they exist, and pretend this was the stone from which the young Arthur pulled out a legendary sword to be revealed as the trueborn heir to the throne.

I've no good reason to suspect it really could be connected with mystical forces and great events from ancient days, or that this place truly is enchanted, but there isn't a smidgen of doubt in my mind about what the poem means by 'King Arthur's magic stone in the fairy glade'. The mystery is how the unknown author knows my private thoughts.

3   The Gifts

It's Saturday, so there's no need to rush off to school, and I open my cards and presents at a special birthday breakfast of fresh orange juice, scrambled eggs and croissants. I decide not to let on about the scroll, and wait to see if anyone else mentions it.

Two small parcels have come for me in the post. Nana and Pa, Mum's parents, have kept their promise to give me a watch, and there is a cool surprise from Gran and Grandpa: a red Swiss Army knife with twelve different gadgets. I examine them one at a time, and the scissors help me undo a large package from Mum and Dad.

'Wow, thank's a lot!' It's what I most wanted: a metal detector. However it's not a toy, and it takes me half an hour to detect a coin that Dad has hidden under a rug. I will need to study the instruction manual and practise before taking it out to search for buried treasure.

Jack and George's joint gift is a brass compass, a reproduction of those used by Victorian explorers; it should come in useful on my treasure hunts.

While my brothers are watching cartoons on television, I enjoy the next couple of hours checking out my presents, calling my grandparents to thank them, acknowledging some e-cards and replying to friends' text messages and online birthday greetings.

However, I just can't get the curious poem out of my mind, and decide to have a go at 'Merlin's' first task: to 'bake a cake with special flour'. I assume the leather pouch contains the mystery extra ingredient: 'my powdered potion'.

I've enjoyed baking since I learnt how to make cupcakes last year, so Mum isn't surprised. 'That's fine as long as you wash up afterwards and don't leave any mess.'

She gets out butter, eggs, sugar, milk and flour and leaves me to get on with it. While I'm stirring them up in a bowl, nobody sees me remove a small bag from my pocket and shake its contents into the mixture, which I then pour into a greased cake tin and put in a medium oven.

At twelve o'clock, while the cake is cooking, I conduct a scientific experiment to check my compass by the sun. I'm gutted to find it's not accurate.

I complain to Dad, who is mowing the lawn. 'Either my new watch or my compass is faulty. My watch says it's midday, but the sun's not due south.'

'I'm sure your compass and watch are both fine,' he reassures me, 'it's our time that's wrong. In spring we put our clocks forward one hour to British Summer Time, and we live a hundred miles west of the Greenwich Meridian where the clocks are set, so here the sun is overhead ten minutes later. Therefore solar noon won't be until ten past one.'

'If we are able to change time, does that mean we can travel through it?' I wonder out loud.

'Yes, we can cross time zones in an aeroplane, and if you were to telephone your Aunt Gwen in California now, you'd be waking her up in the middle of the night.'

'That's not what I mean. Can anyone go back or forward hundreds or thousands of years?' I am thinking about the words on the scroll. 'I'd love to be able to visit Camelot in the days of King Arthur; it must have been wicked there!'

'That's impossible, but it would have been pretty unpleasant and uncomfortable without modern science and technology. You should appreciate how lucky you are to be living here and now.'

I don't agree with him; despite any hardship it must have been brilliant in the company of the Knights of the Round Table.

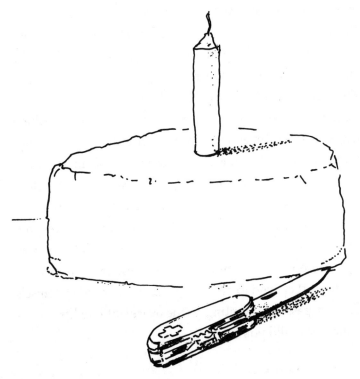

Back in the kitchen I stab my new Swiss Army knife deep into the heart of my cake to test it. No dough sticks to the blade, so I remove the cake from the oven and place it on a metal rack to cool. It's very hard, unlike one of Mum's feather-light Victoria sponges, and I have to use my knife to insert 'Merlin's candle' before hiding the cake in a cupboard.

The highlight of my day is in the afternoon, when my five closest friends are invited to my birthday tea party.

Toby and his sister Anne arrive first and give me a siren for my bike; it has a bright blue, flashing strobe light and sounds like an ambulance on an emergency call. It's so loud that I don't hear the doorbell and am startled when Justin walks in and wishes me many happy returns.

Justin and I go to judo lessons together on Wednesdays after school, and we have both just been awarded our orange belts. Justin is a practical joker, and his present is in character: a battery-powered, electronic snake that slithers across the floor hissing like a live adder. It frightens poor Jasper, who barks furiously until it's switched off.

Sarah lives next door, and her gift is a telescope, which extends to three times its length when pulled open. I look forward to observing the stars through it. Sarah is clever, creative and good at writing poetry, and she therefore has to be my prime suspect as possible author of 'Merlin's Summons'. The clinching factor is that she shares my interest in the Arthurian era, although she resents the way women are portrayed in most of the stories: apart from some evil witches they tend to be '...pathetic, empty-headed damsels in distress, passively awaiting rescue by valiant knights.'

She has a valid point!

Tom arrives late as usual. His present is a useful black rucksack, and all my other gifts go into it apart from the metal detector, which is far too big, and the watch, which I'm wearing on my wrist.

I decide to confront my friends with the scroll, so I can try to guess from their reactions if any of them were responsible for it. Leading them to my desk I remove the key from my pocket and open the middle drawer with a flourish: 'Look what Jasper brought me this morning!'

To my bafflement the drawer is empty apart from some grey dust and a blob of red wax. I have the only key, and the lock hasn't been forced, yet the mystifying parchment has vanished. My first impression is that it has disintegrated into the pile of dust, but I know this is impossible. Such a process would take thousands of years, not just a few hours.

I mumble awkwardly: 'Someone must have moved what I wanted to show you, but it doesn't matter.' Of course it does matter a lot, but I'm not going to spoil the party by making a fuss now. There's no point showing my friends the cake, the candle or the empty pouch that contained the powder; they are meaningless without the evidence of the lost scroll and its enigmatic instructions.

It has left me with three riddles to solve: who sent it, what does it mean and how has it disappeared?

Tea almost makes up for my disappointment. Mum has created a proper birthday cake in the shape of a shield, with a chocolate icing dragon and eleven candles. After a rousing chorus of 'Happy birthday to you', I blow them all out with one huge puff to earn my secret wish: that Merlin's magic really could take me back to Camelot.

4 The Magic

Many years ago my hometown of Sherborne was the capital of the Saxon kingdom of Wessex, the ancient heartland of Southwest England. It is seventeen miles south of Glastonbury, a sacred site of pilgrimage associated with magic and worship since time immemorial, whose ruined medieval abbey was once the richest and grandest monastery in Britain. To my mind the coolest thing about it, though, is its central role in the Arthurian myths and legends.

Between Sherborne and Glastonbury is the Iron Age hill fort of Cadbury Castle. This natural stronghold has long been identified as the probable location of Camelot, although little is known about Britain in 'the Dark Ages', the centuries following the withdrawal of the last Roman legions in the year 410. Historians and archaeologists can't agree where and when King Arthur reigned, or whether he even existed at all, yet I am convinced that the Knights of the Round Table did indeed live very near my home.

Our house, with its creaky, sloping floors, low ceilings and exposed wooden beams, is said to be haunted. I have an unexplainable sixth sense that it's influenced by a paranormal energy coming from the large stone in my secret den, and sometimes when I'm alone there I have strange daydreams about Camelot. Nobody else seems to be affected by it in the same way, so I keep this to myself; I don't want people to think I'm having delusions or going nutty.

Sarah's dad, our neighbour Dr Blore, knows a lot about geology and says that it's a glacial sarsen stone, like those forming the famous, monumental Neolithic stone circles of Avebury and Stonehenge in Wiltshire, the next county.

At six o'clock my friends leave with the usual round of thanks and goodbyes, each clutching a party bag with a slice of birthday cake and a going-home present. I sneak away and remove my own special cake, the peculiar candle and a box of matches from the kitchen cupboard. Then I head for my den with Jasper, determined to carry out all the odd directives in the scroll despite its eerie disappearance.

The presents in my rucksack fulfil the instruction to 'bring such gifts as you can handle'. Of course I don't really expect this performance to lead to 'a great adventure', but only Jasper will witness me making a fool of myself, and he won't be telling anyone.

I put my watch back by one hour and ten minutes to correct for British Summer Time and our being west of Greenwich. It's now set according to the sun, and coming up to 'five hours after noon': the moment for magic specified in the verse.

I place the cake on top of 'King Arthur's magic stone' and cut a slice with my knife. It tastes OK, although it's very hard and solid. Perhaps the 'powdered potion' in the leather pouch contained cement powder!

I strike a match and light the candle. Its pungent scent fills my nostrils and makes me feel light-headed.

Jasper tugs at my shoe with a plaintive whine, so I pick him up and give him a small piece of cake to eat too.

Then, with great difficulty because my mouth is full of cake and my arms are full of dog, I walk backwards three times round the stone, reciting twice on each circuit the mantra in the poem: 'I summon Merlin's magic powers to take me back to Camelot's towers.'

After the third and final circuit I swallow my mouthful of cake, blow out the candle and call out the name 'Merlin' seven times.

I think I've remembered and carried out all the instructions.

A sudden blinding flash forces me to shut my eyes.

I feel dizzy and unbalanced, as if being whirled around on a fairground roundabout, and am deafened by pulsating, high-pitched noises, accelerating as they intensify.

Walking backwards in circles and blowing too hard must have made me giddy.

Are the smelly fumes from the candle affecting me?

Maybe the powder that I added to the cake was a dangerous drug!

While these random thoughts are running through my head, it's hard to stay on my feet and avoid dropping Jasper.

Then the visions, sounds and sensations stop as abruptly as they started. I open my eyes again gingerly and gape in wide-eyed disbelief.

Jasper is still in my arms, while the cake, candle and knife are still on the stone in front of me, but we are no longer in my den. We are inside a primitive wooden hut. The floor is bare earth and there are no windows, although daylight comes in through a hole near the apex of a pitched straw roof. 'King Arthur's magic stone' is no longer half-buried, but standing on top of the ground like a table. It's very confusing and scary, but Jasper's reassuring company stops me from panicking and helps me overcome my anxiety.

I put my things back in the rucksack and listen out for traffic and the familiar noises of home. However the only sounds I can hear are birdsong, trickling water and rustling leaves.

This place is too lifelike to be an illusion, but how could we have been transported somewhere else in a split second?

I'm sure I haven't lost consciousness or been hypnotised. I've never experienced anything so spooky in my life.

5 The Knight

I push the door open and peek outside. Where on earth am I? There's no sign of my home or even of the town of Sherborne. I'm frightened, my heart starts racing and I can't stop trembling. Jasper runs around sniffing, and I can tell he's discombobulated too.

In front of the hut there's a picturesque clearing, surrounded by trees of varied shades of green and carpeted with moss, grass, ferns and a multicoloured profusion of wild flowers. A small waterfall is cascading down a rocky hillside into a clear pool of bright water, illuminated by a ray of sunshine piercing like a spotlight through a gap in the trees.

Gaudy, shimmering butterflies flutter around me, and the birdsongs of thrushes, chirping blackbirds with yellow beaks and red-breasted robins are all competing for attention. The squirrels scampering about in search of food have beautiful brownish red fur, unlike the dull, grey squirrels in our garden. This surreal scene is so colourful and vivid that it's as if I've stepped into an animated computer game.

I can't make sense of it and go right off the idea of 'a great adventure'. I call out anxiously for Mum, Dad, anyone – but there's no answer.

Jasper pricks up his silky brown ears and barks a warning. Then a faint clip-clop rhythm of horse hooves announces an even more improbable sight: a knight in armour on a white horse emerges from a narrow track, shadowed by the trees and dappled with patches of sunlight. His stocky steed has a strange saddle with horned pommels sticking up at the corners and no stirrups. It must be difficult for the rider to control it and not fall off. A long lance is in a holder on the right side of the saddle, and a shield is hooked on the left.

The knight's battered armour isn't bright and shining, but appears more authentic than that at the historical pageant where I saw a medieval jousting tournament re-enacted. A blood-soaked rag is bandaged around his left hand, giving the impression he's been wounded.

A donkey is being led behind the horse by a rope, and both appear worn out and hard-ridden. I doubt if people would pay good money to see a show with animals in such a sorry state.

The knight pulls up in front of the hut and dismounts. His athletic agility in clanking armour is impressive; he must have put in a lot of practice.

He comes over as if he's expecting to find me. 'Are you Master Henry?'

'My name is Henry, but I don't know where we are. Are you sure you're looking for me?'

'How old are you?'

'Eleven; today is my birthday.'

'That is the answer Lord Merlin said you would give, so you must be the lad I was sent to meet. Climb up onto the donkey and we can be on our way.'

He bends to pat Jasper, who wags his tail. 'Is this little creature with you?'

'Yes, he's my dog Jasper. But who are you and where do you want to take us?'

'I am Sir Perceval from the Fellowship of the Round Table, and we must proceed forthwith to Camelot.'

I take a deep breath and manage to overcome my anxiety enough to enter into the spirit of his charade: 'Oh, are we going to King Arthur's Court?'

'Yes, of course,' answers the knight in a matter-of-fact, deadpan way, as though stating something obvious and normal. 'Lord Merlin and the King are expecting you this evening.'

The many warnings from my teachers and parents never to accept lifts from strangers spring to my mind: 'How do I know I can trust you?'

The knight points at the shield fixed to his horse's saddle. 'Lord Merlin advised me you should recognise this emblem.'

The red crest on his white shield looks familiar; it is like the fire-breathing dragon embossed on the wax seal of the peculiar scroll.

'Hurry up, we must leave here at once,' the knight stresses with a sense of urgency. 'Sir Mordred's army is encamped less than an hour's march away. You don't want to hang around and risk falling into their hands, do you?'

Something about his tone of voice makes me reluctant to find out, even though his ridiculous threat is so fake.

I've often promised never to get into a stranger's car, but nobody ever said anything about a donkey.

Jasper likes this man, and as a rule his instincts are reliable, except for his uncharacteristic aggression towards postmen.

It's a good thing that a suit of armour doesn't have the same effect on him as a Royal Mail uniform.

With no clue as to my whereabouts or how to find my way home, I'll have to go along with this pretend knight for the time being; so I climb up onto the donkey as instructed.

In fact I'm starting to enjoy my incredible predicament, but suspect it has to be a dream. If it is, then I hope I don't wake up quite yet, in case I'm unable to get back into it again.

6   The Forest

A damp blanket of cold fog swirls up suddenly from the pool and rolls across the clearing in deepening waves. There's something unnatural about it that chills me to the core of my being.

The birds squawk in alarm and then go quiet, as the atmosphere is transformed in seconds from entrancing beauty into obscure gloom. I haven't seen such dense fog even in winter, and certainly never in summer, and can barely make out the hut a few yards away. These unfamiliar surroundings felt welcoming a moment ago, but have become sinister and menacing.

A harsh screech pierces through the silence with a jolt. Jasper stands rigid with his tail sticking up like a flagpole, instinctively on guard.

The knight looks worried and makes the sign of a cross for protection. 'That's the cry of a black carrion crow, the bird of death and witchcraft; it tells me that this miasma has been conjured up by foul sorcery to entrap or delay us. Camelot stands two leagues to the north, but we dare not try to make our way there now. Travellers have been rumoured to vanish without a trace in this enchanted forest. Despite the danger we'll have to stay here until it clears, even though Lord Merlin is waiting for you.'

'How far is a league?'

'A league is the distance of an hour's normal walk, about three Roman miles,' answers the man who calls himself Sir Perceval.

He notices that I am shivering, and produces an old cloak from the donkey's saddlebag for me to wear over my shorts and T-shirt. It is made of coarse wool and is more or less the right size; I put it on thankfully, even though it smells of sweat and horses and can't have been in a washing machine for ages.

Then I remember the compass among my birthday presents, take it out of the rucksack and consult it. 'I can find our route through the fog; we need to go that way.'

I point north and show my compass to the knight, who eyeballs it in bafflement as if he's never seen anything like it.

'Merlin said you come from an exotic land and possess great knowledge despite your tender age. If you believe you can guide us through this obscurity with your perplexing device, then I'll take my chances with you. I am a knight, skilled in arms and dedicated to chivalry, but I know nothing about divination or the mystery of books.'

'Are you saying you can't read?' I blurt out.

He doesn't seem at all fazed by my tactlessness.

'Certainly not, I'm a fighter not a scholar. Come on young Henry, let's be on our way.'

The cheery knight in armour sets off at a steady walk on his white charger, leading my donkey behind. I call out directions and Jasper runs alongside.

He seems a nice man, and I enquire about the bloodied rag around his hand: 'Have you hurt yourself?'

'It's only a scratch. I bumped into two enemy scouts on my way to meet you. I killed one and the other ran away, but then the coward shot an arrow at me from behind and grazed me.'

The blood makes this outrageous and far-fetched explanation sound almost plausible.

We make good progress northwards until Sir Perceval pulls to an abrupt halt. 'We will have to dismount, my horse has gone lame.'

A stone in its hoof has caused the problem, and I save the day with another of my presents: a spike on the Swiss army knife. I demonstrate some of its other gadgets to the knight, who couldn't appear more incredulous if I'd landed from another planet on a flying saucer or had two heads. I almost laugh out loud at his theatrical performance, which is far too exaggerated to be convincing.

We remount and are about to set off again when a bloodcurdling howl echoes out of the ghostly mist. I shudder and can't help shaking, the horse becomes jumpy and agitated, and even the fearless Jasper tries to hide between the donkey's legs.

'I hope that is just an ordinary wolf, but I suspect it's a werewolf,' says the knight. This is even more implausible, as I know there haven't been any wolves in Southern England outside zoos for hundreds of years, and I've never heard of werewolves anywhere except Transylvania. However, I am anxious to escape from this depressing forest as soon as possible. I have to admit that the howl sounded far too real for my liking, and I can't avoid a creepy sensation that evil eyes are observing us from the murky shadows.

We ride on at an accelerated pace until, to my profound relief, we emerge from the oppressive gloom into brightness and light, and the fog evaporates as fast as it arrived. My watch says it's just after six o'clock, an hour since we set off. The sun is shining from a clear blue sky and birds are singing again.

Ahead of us looms a huge castle on the top of a fortified hill with steep sides about three hundred feet high. There is a moat in front of a wooden palisade around the foot of the hill, and behind it a track winds up the slopes to the massive walls encircling the summit. The grey stone ramparts appear sturdy and powerful, and they are brightened by lots of colourful flags and banners fluttering on turrets and spires.

'There stands King Arthur's great stronghold of Camelot,' Sir Perceval declares. 'I cannot comprehend how you managed to guide us through the bewitched mist.'

I put my compass away with pride, enjoying the praise but puzzled how to make sense of where we are. Six miles north of my home is Cadbury Castle, long considered to be the likely location of Camelot – but that was around fifteen centuries ago.

The hill in front of me is of a similar shape and size to Cadbury Castle, which my class visited on a school field trip. However Cadbury's slopes are densely wooded, and no trace remains of its ancient fortifications, while this place has walls and buildings on it and far fewer trees.

We are in open countryside, the air smells fresh and clean, and there's no traffic noise or pollution. There is no sign of the nearby villages of Queen Camel and West Camel, whose names underline the local claim to a Camelot connection.

The weirdest thing about this conundrum, though, is that the fortress in front of me isn't a ruined monument like the Norman and medieval castles near my home and in many parts of Britain; it appears to be a vibrant, living place.

7   The Castle

We approach the fortifications at the bottom of the hill, and the knight sounds a shrill note on a hunting horn followed by a shout: 'Make passage for Sir Perceval.'

With a rattle of chains a creaking drawbridge is lowered to let us cross over the moat. This place looks far more solid and real than a theme park, and it's even more convincing than the special effects of the fog and those bloodcurdling howls in the forest.

The guards who man the walls return Sir Perceval's wave, and we pass a hotchpotch of huts, workshops, stables and stinking sheds. Labourers are working with wooden pitchforks, dressed in loose smocks that hang down to their knees.

A cobbled track takes us up the hill to the summit and the fortified outer gateway, a ten-foot-wide restricted space surrounded by high walls on all sides. Sir Perceval points out where archers can shoot arrows from small holes and defenders can drop boiling oil or rocks onto the heads of unwelcome visitors.

We ride under a raised portcullis and emerge onto a domed plateau similar in size to Cadbury Castle, which according to my history teacher has an area of eighteen acres and a perimeter of three quarters of a mile. Soldiers are patrolling along a wooden walkway behind crenellated ramparts, dressed more like Roman legionaries than medieval troops and armed with short swords or bows.

Huge catapults with weights and coiled ropes are strategically placed on towers at intervals around the walls, which have rooms and workshops built within them. Sir Perceval explains: 'Those mighty weapons are ballistae, and they can hurl stone balls accurately for great distances.'

Could this be a film set for a period drama? Everything I've ever been taught makes me certain it can't possibly be real, but all my senses are telling me that it is.

It isn't a farmyard, but there are plenty of unusual domestic animals, like those at the farm park that preserves rare native breeds: speckled pigs with rings through their snouts, black hens with short legs in pens beside ducks with shiny green heads, and long-haired grey goats tethered to stakes as living lawnmowers to keep the grass down.

We cross the plateau at a leisurely pace, passing timber houses with steep, thatched roofs and a few stone buildings, including a chapel with a big cross outside. We are heading towards the turreted castle that dominates this walled settlement.

I see a bustling open-air market, where strange artefacts, outlandish clothes, leather belts, wooden bowls, pots, metal knives and peculiar utensils are displayed, alongside loaves of black bread, cheese, drinks in ceramic pots, jars of honey, nuts and grains.

Women dressed in little more than rags are selling produce from open baskets – one shouts 'Oysters, live oysters,' and another offers us bunches of herbs.

People are wearing very odd outfits, particularly the headgear. In the crowd are several monks in brown hooded cowls, ladies with white scarves suspended from tall, pointed hats, and men with soft, cone-shaped caps. All the clothes are made of dull, plain material without any patterns or pockets. Most men have wide leather belts with metal buckles and clips, from which they hang their tools, knives and purses.

The sentries at the gateway of the fairy-tale castle salute Sir Perceval as we enter a large courtyard. A young boy of around my age in a plain yellow tunic runs up and greets us. He has a mop of scraggly brown hair, bright blue eyes and dirty fingernails.

He holds the horse and donkey steady while we climb down, and the knight introduces us: 'This is Luke – my trainee squire. Luke, Master Henry is a traveller from afar here to visit Lord Merlin, and his strange hound is called Jasper.'

Luke strokes my dog and smiles at me as he helps unbuckle and remove Sir Perceval's cumbersome armour. I think we'll get on.

Without his armour the knight looks rather ordinary; he is short and muscular and is wearing a knee-length, long-sleeved tunic. He instructs Luke to get the animals watered, fed and groomed, and then to go and clean his armour and weapons.

'Please come with me, Master Henry – Lord Merlin is awaiting you.'

We cross the courtyard, enter a doorway at the base of a tall circular tower, and climb up a stone spiral staircase lit by burning torches. Shafts of light filter through narrow slits in the walls, and beside each one is a kind of umbrella stand full of arrows. At the top of the stairs there is a heavy oak door with a knocker carved in the shape of a hand.

Sir Perceval raps twice, and a muffled voice calls out: 'Enter.'

8 The Wizard

Sir Perceval ushers me into a dark, gloomy room about twenty feet wide. Rush mats cover the rough wood floor, and the walls are bare and undecorated, apart from a hanging tapestry depicting a rampant dragon surrounded by curious symbols. A small window overlooks the courtyard; it has unpainted shutters but no glass, blinds or curtains.

The furniture consists of a four-poster bed with an animal-skin rug but no pillows or sheets, a heavy wooden table, a chest of drawers, a couple of three-legged stools and several candlesticks. There isn't a sink or basin, but there are some leather buckets of water and a half-full chamber pot.

Open shelves over a fireplace display a hotchpotch of jars and flasks, whose weird ingredients are labelled in alphabetical order from 'adders' tongues' to 'unicorn horn', with 'mandrake root' and 'mistletoe' near the middle. There's a motley collection of ghoulish objects, including skulls, bats' wings, dried lizards and toads.

As my eyes wander round the room, I spy various tools and implements: a stone mortar and pestle, a set of bone-handled knives and some simple scales.

A cauldron of treacly liquid is bubbling on a stand over a candle inside the fireplace alcove. It smells like the 'powdered potion' that I put into the cake.

On the table are three large hand-written books, a few sheets of animal-skin parchment, a feather quill pen and an inkwell. The parchment and the handwriting remind me of the bizarre scroll that set off all these weird happenings.

A tall, thin old man with a hooked nose is standing in the middle of the room. He's leaning on a thick staff with elaborate carvings and a handle shaped like a dragon's head. His white beard is almost as long as his hooded robe, but he has a kind face, although he looks frail and weary.

'Welcome Master Henry, I am Merlin. I am very pleased to make your acquaintance and delighted you managed to accept my invitation and come here.'

I am lost for words. How can this possibly be the world-famous wizard in person?

Merlin turns to the knight. 'Thank you, Sir Perceval, for bringing my young visitor from the enchanted forest. I am sure you want to go and prepare yourself for tonight's feast, but please send young Luke here to show our guest around.'

Sir Perceval leaves with a nod and a smile towards me. Then I ask the obvious question, trying to conceal my nervousness and to sound polite and respectful.

'Please, Sir, where am I?'

'You are not very far from your home in distance,' is the old man's cryptic reply. 'However, you should be asking when am I? rather than where am I?'

'I don't understand what you mean, Sir, so please will you explain everything to me?'

'I can't possibly explain everything,' says Merlin in an irritated way, as if exasperated by such a stupid question, 'but I will explain something. You are in Camelot at the Court of Arthur Pendragon, the High King of Britain. If my spell has worked as intended, then you have travelled not to a different place but to another time. Am I right to believe that you are from the dawning of the third millennium?'

'Yes, if that's what you call the twenty-first century. But what are you saying the date is now?'

'Today...,' Merlin pauses for effect, 'it is two days after the Ides of June in the year of Our Lord 533.'

'That's impossible,' I interrupt in stunned disbelief.

'No, it's not,' snaps the wizard. 'You're here, aren't you? Your presence is the result of my magical experiment to try to safeguard the achievements of King Arthur and protect Camelot from a dreadful threat. I am gratified that you and your odd little hound have arrived here undamaged. This is the first occasion I have succeeded in conjuring up such a transmogrification.'

I don't like the sound of this at all. 'He is my Jack Russell terrier, Jasper. But what on earth is a transmogi-fixation?'

'A transmogrification is a change of place, nature or time in a magical and surprising manner. I still haven't discovered why it's never worked before, but a portal or doorway in time only opens on very rare occasions for a brief moment. At last I appear to have managed to identify the precise place and instant to effect a temporal transmogrification, a leap across time. Many congratulations on your able assistance at the other end of the chronological portal. It can only have succeeded because you must have followed all my instructions and pronounced my spell with heartfelt sincerity.'

'Why have you summoned me here? I am just an ordinary schoolboy, so how can I help you protect Camelot?'

'You were identified and located in the future by King Arthur's magic stone, and it was prophesied by the runes. I admit I was dumbfounded to learn that so young a boy was the helper from another era selected by the fates for this critical task.'

'Who are the runes?'

'Runes are not people,' laughs Merlin. 'They form part of an ancient and secret rite of the Norse and Germanic tribes, in which sacred symbols are marked on tablets of stone, wood and bone. When we cast them to the ground, the spirits sometimes reveal their messages to us. These oracles are known as runecasts. I am pleased you were able to perform the steps in my summons; I tried to make it clear and simple for you.'

'In that case why did you write it in verse? It would have been easier to follow your instructions if they had been in normal sentences,' I tell him.

'I don't know why, but my spells seem to work better when they rhyme. Also divination mustn't be too easy to understand, since familiarity detracts from the wonderment. Imagine, for example, if a wizard were to create a candle that can light a room for weeks without burning up, construct a conveyance that enables men to fly, or find a way to converse with the inhabitants of a distant land. Even such inconceivable sorcery would cease to be thought of as magic if people got used to it.'

I nod, knowing that all these inventions are everyday items taken for granted in my world.

9 The Spell

'Please, Sir, how are Jasper and I going to get back home again?' I ask the wizard, hoping for a simple solution to my predicament.

'According to the auguries of the runes and my detailed calculations, the portal in time will be open once more at noon tomorrow in the same enchanted place. If you want to pass back through it, you will need to light my candle again on top of the magical stone and take another bite of your cake containing my potion; then you should walk three times around the stone, facing forwards and in the opposite direction to before, and say twice on each circuit: "I summon Merlin's magic powers to return me to my home and proper time." After that swallow the cake, blow out the candle and again call out my name seven times.'

Merlin suddenly looks anxious. 'Fiddlesticks and botheration! I may have neglected to inform you that it's essential to employ the same cake and candle if you want to reverse the spell and travel back to the future. Do you still have them in your possession?'

I check in my rucksack and nod. He appears relieved and mumbles: 'That's fortunate; I am getting a trifle forgetful these days.' This doesn't inspire me with much confidence in his ability to send us back where we belong.

'Excuse me, but your spell doesn't rhyme, and yet you told me just now that your spells work better when they rhyme.'

'Yes, you are correct,' Merlin acknowledges grudgingly, 'but I am very tired and can't think of an appropriate word to fit the context and rhyme with powers.'

'How about hours?'

'That's good! I will change the incantation as you suggest, and instead you can recite the spell: "I summon Merlin's magic power to take me home this very hour."'

'On reflection it's more likely to be efficacious. Even King Arthur wouldn't presume to advise me how to compose an enchantment, so it makes a refreshing change to meet someone who questions everything. I am at last beginning to understand why you might have been chosen. Tell me, have you brought any paranormal accoutrements here to Camelot?'

'I don't think so; what are they?' I haven't a clue what he's getting at.

'Miraculous devices or supernatural paraphernalia,' the wizard elaborates without making himself much clearer.

'I only have my birthday presents,' I apologise.

'Show me!' commands the sorcerer in an urgent, imperious tone of voice.

I open my rucksack and lay the contents out on the table.

'Excellent, excellent. These are all potent, mystic instruments, since none of them will be invented for many centuries to come. They can be of great assistance if you employ them with wisdom and discretion.'

He examines my collection of objects with curiosity and extraordinary enthusiasm, as animated as a young boy in a toyshop. He presses a button on the siren and jumps back in alarm at the alien electronic sound of an ambulance and the sight of a blue, flashing strobe light. I have to switch it off for him, because Merlin hasn't a clue how to do it.

My wristwatch fascinates him. 'How ingenious, what an astonishing chronometer. It should enable you to identify with precision the auspicious instant to work the magic, tomorrow at noon. This must be far more accurate than a sundial and even work on cloudy days and at night.'

He demonstrates his own timepiece; it's an adjustable bronze ring hanging from a cord with a small hole, through which the sun can reflect on Roman numerals engraved inside.

'You'll need a tinderbox to light the magic candle, as I notice that you don't have one,' Merlin announces.

'It's alright, I've got a box of matches.' I strike one as a demonstration.

'That wondrous fire stick is amazing!' Merlin looks seriously impressed. It has never occurred to me that a simple match might be considered a mind-blowing invention.

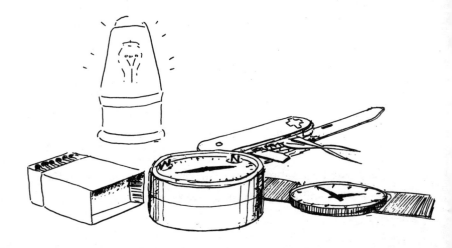

'These astounding appliances can be of great help to you on your mission,' Merlin remarks.

'Mission? Did you say mission?' I ask nervously.

'Yes, of course. I only summoned you here because there's an important task for which you are destined; King Arthur will give you the details this evening. Now please pay careful attention to some crucial advice: first, do not show these futuristic inventions to anyone unless it is essential; second, on no account leave any of them here where they don't belong, or unpredictable consequences could ensue; and third tell no one that you are a visitor from the future. It must remain our private secret how you come to be in Camelot. Even Sir Perceval mustn't know your origin; he's a regular, straightforward knight and would be alarmed by the truth. I took the precaution of advising him that you might be a bit confused, in case you said anything to alert him.'

'I can still hardly accept that I'm in the past, and we didn't discuss the date, so I doubt if he suspects I've come from the future. However, I've always been taught to tell the truth; are you saying that's wrong?'

'I'm not saying it's wrong,' Merlin replies in a slow and deliberate way, 'but it might be more prudent to tell people what they can comprehend, if you wish to avoid difficulties and undesirable complications. Nobody would believe the truth, and I would have to deny any involvement in such forbidden forms of sorcery; so they'd either lock you up as a lunatic if you're lucky, or test you for witchcraft if you're not.'

'How do they do that?'

'As a rule they submit you to an ordeal by water. They tie you to a stool and duck you under water in a pond for longer than any normal person can hold their breath,' elaborates the wizard. 'If you are still alive when they take you out, they assume that you must be a witch to have survived and burn you at the stake. If you drown, they acknowledge you weren't a witch after all. It's too late to bring you back to life, but at least they give you a decent burial, properly aligned from north to south if you are a pagan, or west to east if you are a Christian, so you can still have a chance of an afterlife.'

'What should I say to avoid being accused of being a witch?' I ask in horror, not ready to be buried facing either direction.

'You'd better pretend you are from across the sea, on the way from Armorica in northwest Gaul to the Great Stone Circle of Stonehenge for next week's summer solstice. That should avoid suspicion, because weird characters in outlandish clothes often turn up there for the midsummer festival. Nobody ever knows where they all arrive from or disappear to again afterwards.

'If you are brave and pure in heart, then you may succeed in your mission and return to the future, and your reward will be beyond your wildest expectations. However, no one will believe that you have visited us in Camelot.

'I regret that if you fail and can't reverse the spell at the appointed place and hour, then you will simply have to stay here for the rest of your life. You might get used to it after a while if you survive your quest – though it must be much more primitive and less comfortable than life in your century.'

I always wanted to visit Camelot, but never for a single moment considered being marooned there.

I start to picture my parents' distress if Jasper and I were to vanish without a trace and never be seen or heard from again. This adventure is turning into the most horrific nightmare.

10 The Traveller

It was always my ultimate fantasy to visit the Court of King Arthur, but it never involved being stranded for life. Now my sole ambition is to turn the clock back, or rather forward, so I can go home. I've no interest in the prospect of a reward, but if I am to see my family again I suppose I'll have to do exactly what Merlin says.

I'm putting my belongings back into my rucksack when he adds: 'You should not fear our different way of being, but you must always stand apart from ordinary people here, and be conscious that you are a wizard.'

'No, I'm not,' I protest. 'You must have mixed me up with someone else and summoned the wrong person to Camelot; I know nothing at all about wizardry.'

'Oh, but you do,' insists Merlin in a reassuring voice. 'You recognised and invoked the magic of the stone, you are familiar with things that haven't yet existed and you know answers to mysteries never revealed to any living man. Such information gives you immense authority and influence, for no divination is greater than a knowledge of the future.'

While I'm trying to figure out how any of this could help me, there is a timid knock.

'Enter,' calls Merlin.

The door creaks open, and in walks Sir Perceval's young squire Luke.

'You sent for me, Lord Merlin?'

'Have you met our visitor, Master Henry?'

Luke nods. 'Yes, my Lord.'

'Good. Please show him and his odd little hound around Camelot and bring them to the banquet in the Great Hall at sunset. Master Henry is to sit at your table.'

Merlin turns to me. 'I won't be attending tonight's feast because I dislike rowdy crowds and noise. If all goes to plan, we won't need to meet again. Take care to follow my advice and to heed my warnings. If you do so and use your wits, then you have a reasonable chance of getting home again safely. Good luck, Henry.'

He shakes my hand and pats Jasper, but doesn't sound convinced. I don't feel at all encouraged by his minimal instructions and apparent lack of certainty.

Luke and I leave the main castle for a tour around Camelot. The unaccustomed sights and sounds are so fascinating that I forget about my predicament for a while, and Jasper relishes sniffing out lots of unfamiliar smells.

First we climb up to the wall-walk behind the parapet on the ramparts. Silhouetted against a red sky over the battlements is a distant rainbow, and at its end is a steep, pointed hill. A track leads northwest towards it across level moorlands.

'That is the holy hill of Glastonbury,' Luke points out. 'King Arthur has built a fort there to protect the new monastery and abbey. In return for our protection the monks supply Camelot with luxuries such as salt and preserved fish. They also distil an alcoholic liqueur from herbs that helps reduce the pain from battle wounds, but it's appreciated a bit too much and too often by one or two of the knights, though I'd better not name them.'

'Why is the hill holy?'

'The abbey is next to a hallowed thorn tree that grew out of the staff of Joseph of Arimathea, the saint who buried Jesus. They say he came here from Jerusalem almost five hundred years ago with the Holy Grail, the cup from which our Lord drank at the last supper. Sir Perceval has had a vision about it and has dedicated his life to recovering the lost Grail.

'The religious origins of Glastonbury go back long before Christianity, however. There's a prehistoric stone circle of the sun around St Michael's Tower on top of Glastonbury Tor, and hidden in the nearby marshes and lagoons lies the Isle of Avalon, the forbidden land of the dead. That is where our King's sword Excalibur was forged by the Lady of the Lake.'

Then Luke adds in an ominous whisper: 'They say the Lord of the Underworld and King of the Fairies, Gwyn ap Nudd, used to live at Glastonbury until a Christian monk defeated and expelled him. Many people still fear the old gods will prove stronger than the monks and that the forces of darkness will soon shroud the land once more.'

This all sounds very spooky, but so too is my knowledge that the monastery will flourish for another thousand years, until its abbey is dissolved and utterly destroyed in the sixteenth century by King Henry the Eighth.

'I hope you don't mind having to show me round,' I apologise to Luke.

'Far from it. Thanks to your being here, today someone else is having to clean Sir Perceval's armour and groom his horse.'

There are wicker cages at intervals around the walls, each containing several small, white tufted geese. 'Those are our guard geese; they honk to warn us if intruders approach from outside at night,' Luke explains, surprised that I'm only familiar with guard dogs and not geese.

The stinking cloak that I'm wearing over my own clothes makes me look less of an oddity; however there are a few stares when anyone notices my shorts and trainers. Boys here wear tunics and flat leather sandals, held on by thongs tied round their ankles and legs.

To my relief everyone is more interested in Jasper than in me or my clothes. He is far cuter than any of the local hunting dogs, and more obedient and intelligent. People are impressed by his friendliness and by the way he sits or offers his paw when told.

Luke stops to chat to occasional passing acquaintances, introducing me as a traveller from across the sea. This accounts for my abnormal outfit, and no one asks me where I'm from.

'Do you want to become a knight when you grow up?' I enquire.

'Fat chance I've got. I'm not of noble birth and so can only be made a knight in very exceptional circumstances. My father is just a free yeoman, although he has worked hard and owns his farm. My ambition is to become a minstrel and compose ballads about the knights and their exploits; I am learning to play the lyre. Do you like music?'

'Yes. I play the saxophone and my brother is learning the piano.'

The blank expression on Luke's face prompts me to explain that a saxophone is a metal wind instrument with a wooden reed. My attempts to describe a piano are less successful until he shows a faint glimmer of recognition. 'Is it something like a big dulcimer?'

I nod without knowing what this is, and he seems pleased to have identified it.

'A celebrated Celtic troubadour is coming to perform his latest ballad to the Court at this evening's banquet; if you appreciate good music you couldn't have arrived on a better day. Have you come across the minstrel Taliesin of Caerleon on your travels?'

'No, but I look forward to hearing him.'

'You must be ever so courageous to visit other lands,' Luke states. 'I hope that one day I might go abroad on a pilgrimage to a holy shrine.'

Being used to the comfort of cars, trains or aeroplanes, I've never considered you need to be brave to travel, except when my grandfather is driving without paying attention, which can be nerve-racking for passengers and other road users. The notion of going hundreds of miles just for a holiday, in a few hours' air-conditioned luxury instead of many hazardous and exhausting weeks on foot or horseback, would be unimaginable to anyone here.

I am stunned to learn that there isn't a school in Camelot. Living here might have certain advantages in spite of the chores of cleaning armour; at least there can't be any homework.

We pass some barbers and see a monk having a haircut, which involves putting a pudding bowl on his head level with his ears and shaving off all the hair visible around it.

'Barbers are very important,' Luke informs me. 'They don't just shave beards and cut hair, they are also the surgeons who treat you if you have toothache or get injured in battle.'

A man is having a tooth extracted with a large pair of pliers, and his horrifying yells make me realise that I shouldn't complain about having a pain-killing injection when I go to the dentist.

There are moments when I still suspect that this entire surreal experience must be a vivid dream, but there's no escaping from it. I try a hard pinch on my hand; it hurts but doesn't wake me up.

11 The Fortress

Theres nothing more to the famous royal fortress of Camelot than this hilltop settlement and castle, with a few workshops, huts and farm buildings at the foot of the slope.

Crops are growing outside the protected area, and domestic animals graze nearby. It's almost sunset, and Luke points out sheep, goats and cows being herded inside the lower fortifications to be milked and kept safe overnight from outlaws, wolves and other predators. The cattle have short legs and big horns, and the small sheep are dark brown.

'They provide milk, meat, leather and wool, and we make good use of their horns, skin, fat and bones; no part goes to waste,' Luke tells me. 'The King has decreed that animal slaughter and its related, foul-smelling trades must be conducted down at the bottom of the hill, so up here we are spared from the stench of tanning, tallow chandlers making candles from fat, and glue-makers boiling up animal bones.'

I ask why there are so many cone-shaped beehives dotted around the slopes. 'Bees make the honey that we use to sweeten food and drink, to cure sicknesses and to brew mead. Also their honeycombs produce sealing wax, skin ointment and the polish that bowyers rub into longbows for strength and flexibility, which gives our archers much greater range and accuracy.'

I remember the Bible's description of the Promised Land as 'flowing with milk and honey', and for the first time understand why that must have been such a good thing.

'Don't you sweeten your food with sugar?'

'I have heard of sugarcane juice from the Indies, which is dried and made into crystals, but so rare a confection can only be afforded by kings and lords. I've never tasted such a delicacy.'

Specialist craftsmen are manufacturing a variety of items in workshops built within the outer defences under the wall-walk, and Luke identifies the different occupations as we pass. Most people labour alone or with one young assistant.

Weavers are interweaving fabrics on wooden looms to make cloth, and dyers are dipping yarn and material in vats of coloured liquid. 'The identity of the roots, plants, crushed insects, minerals and shells for each colour are passed down from fathers to sons,' Luke explains.

It has never occurred to me that this might be a valuable trade secret, but on reflection I wouldn't have a clue what ingredients could dye clothes permanently.

We come to a woodworking area, where wheelwrights are constructing cartwheels and coopers are assembling oak barrels. Carpenters are turning, carving, joining and waxing timber to make spear shafts, axe handles and other implements. They achieve incredible results with their simple hand tools, small bench saws and lathes turned by pedals.

In another sector smoke is rising from many small furnaces. There's a deafening metallic hammering of blacksmiths, working on anvils at red-hot forges to create a fearsome array of lethal weapons: double-headed axes, pikes, spears, maces and daggers. They wear thick leather aprons and gloves, but don't have earplugs, safety goggles or any other protective clothing.

Farriers are making or repairing horseshoes, while armourers are producing shields, helmets and armour. Cutlers are alternately heating and beating steel swords and knives, or sharpening them on rotating, water-cooled grindstones.

Horners are cleaning, curing and polishing animal horns to make drinking vessels, and potters are turning clay pots on wheels or baking the finished products in charcoal-fired kilns.

Luke introduces me to his friend Sam, who is helping his father make wooden arrows, a job known as fletching. Most craftsmen don't have surnames and are simply known by their profession – so he is called 'Sam, the Fletcher'.

'Women are rarely allowed to become apprentices or learn most occupations,' Luke tells me as we pass a group of women bending strips of willow into wickerwork baskets, 'but basket weaving is one of the few crafts suitable for them. They are not skilful or strong enough for manly occupations.'

The equal opportunities and anti-discrimination laws in modern Britain would have astonished Luke, but I keep this to myself.

A visit to the toilet proves embarrassing. Luke directs me to 'the lavatorium', a room with a long wooden bench that has four seats with holes the size of dinner plates. There is no privacy and you have to sit in public over a stinking trench, with lots of flies buzzing around. Luckily no one else is using it, but without disinfectant or running water I almost throw up from the smell. I don't appreciate having to use scratchy leaves instead of soft loo paper.

There are buckets full of wee, and Luke explains that this is always collected and saved, as it has special qualities and is used for tanning leather, to bleach clothes white, as a medicine and, to my disgust, as a beauty product for whitening teeth.

'The lavatorium is nicknamed "the gong",' Luke announces when I emerge holding my nose. 'The wretched serfs who have to clean it are called "gong farmers"; their job is to empty the contents of the trench in buckets and put it on dung heaps to become a fertiliser for our crops.'

'Who are serfs?'

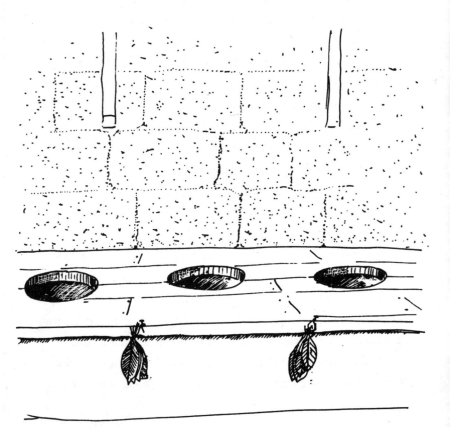

'Serfs are poor peasants who are not freemen and have no skilled craft. They are labourers without land and are bonded to a lord, who gives them subsistence, protection and shelter in return for menial work. We don't keep slaves like the Romans, and serfs have a right to justice from the King, so their lord doesn't have absolute power of life and death over them as in the old days,' Luke elaborates. 'But when serfs are old or become sick and can no longer work, they find it hard to survive the winter. We'd like to help them, but most are too ignorant or stupid to learn new skills. Few live to more than forty years of age.'

This short life expectancy brings home to me that apart from Merlin I haven't seen any old people at Camelot. This place seems very unfair, with prejudices against women and unskilled workers, and no pensions, healthcare or social services. Noble birth is the main qualification for becoming a knight, and with little education there is not much chance to improve your position in society.

It's not a golden age compared with the democratic welfare state where I live, and there are no hospitals or schools. Luke tells me that the King's word is absolute law, and the main concerns are about the basic struggle to survive. With no democracy or elections, people simply look to the King and his knights to tell them what to do and to protect them from enemies.

A stone trough where horses drink is the only place to wash my hands. There is a ball of unscented, rough soap, which Luke explains is a mixture of fat and ashes.

A young, fair-haired girl comes up to us; she's about my age and has a freckled face and an infectious, friendly smile.

Luke introduces her. 'This is my sister Elaine, who works in Queen Guinevere's royal household; the Queen took a liking to her when she went to the palace to deliver honey from my father's farm. It's an honoured position, since most girls are only allowed to work as domestic servants or help their families until they marry. Of course you have a completely different life if you are of high birth or a princess.'

Elaine's dress is little better than a sack, with a hole for her head to go through and a rope belt around her waist. The styling of clothes at Camelot is unimpressive: there are certainly no designer labels or waterproof fabrics, and I doubt if anyone even wears underpants.

'Where do you go to have a bath?' I ask.

'The Romans used to take baths, but we don't do that sort of thing any more these days; they say it isn't healthy or good for you to wet your skin too often.'

Elaine has a feisty attitude and reminds me of my friend Sarah, who would be pleased to know that at least one girl in Camelot has some spirit and independence. She butts in: 'Queen Guinevere takes baths. She makes her servants heat water in a cauldron over a fire and carry buckets of hot water up to a tub in her bedchamber, where her ladies in waiting can bathe her with scented flower petals. She is obsessed with cleanliness and bathes every few months, whether she needs it or not. It serves little purpose, but if you are a queen you are entitled to such extravagant luxuries.'

It's no wonder these people look dirty to my eyes, although their smell certainly appeals to Jasper.

12 The Hall

L uke makes a first-class tour guide. When he isn't pointing out places and items of interest, or explaining who people are and what they are doing, he tells me stories about the heroic feats of the valiant Knights of the Round Table. His tales aren't supernatural like the Arthurian myths in books and films, but without so much sorcery and enchantment the exploits sound far more realistic and exciting.

At sunset a loud bell rings to announce supper, and Luke ushers me into the Great Hall, a large, timber-roofed building with wide, high gables at the centre of the main castle of Camelot. Elaine says goodbye at the door, as she has to go upstairs and sit in a separate ladies' gallery.

Luke asks if I've seen such a fabulous building on my travels.

'It's very splendid,' I respond tactfully, although I am used to seeing ordinary churches that are bigger and more imposing. Nonetheless the banners and armour hanging on the walls are very striking and evocative, especially the axes and the colourful painted shields. The flickering light of hundreds of candles, suspended from the roof beams on iron candelabras, reflects on the shiny steel weapons and causes grotesque carvings of gargoyles near the ceiling to cast eerie moving shadows, lending a dramatic and spectral aura to the hall.

'Tonight we're having a banquet to commemorate the twentieth anniversary of the battle of Mount Badon, when King Arthur defeated the heathen Saxon invaders from across the seas and brought peace and tranquillity to his realm. They say our great king slew nine hundred Saxons with his sword Excalibur that day. The Saxons are still so frightened of him that they haven't dared attack us again since,' Luke announces.

He points out the famous Round Table on a raised platform at the far end of the hall. Tough-looking, scar-faced men occupy about half of the thirty or more seats around it. The seats are called sieges, and most have a name or crest engraved on the back. The table is painted with bright, heraldic designs.

These renowned Knights of the Round Table don't look at all refined or gentlemanly.

I notice Sir Perceval and wave at him, but he acknowledges my greeting with a curt nod and looks away again. I hope I wasn't being disrespectful.

'Why are so many of the sieges empty?'

'Some knights errant are away fighting wars or on quests, and a couple of places belong to kings of other lands, who don't often come to take up their honorary seats at the Round Table. However, our knights are now being killed off faster than we can train or recruit new ones, even though the qualifying standards have been relaxed and are much less strict than they used to be.'

Camelot is much smaller than I expected, so I ask Luke why it is so important.

'Camelot means more as an idea than as a place; it is inspirational because of what it represents. The ethos of the Fellowship of the Round Table is to fight with chivalry and honour to right wrongs, maintain peace and justice, and defend the weak from barbarism and evil. We are so lucky to live in this golden age of order and prosperity. Outside this kingdom there has been no effective law or civilisation in Britain since the Roman legions left more than a hundred years ago and the savage barbarians invaded.

'Thanks to our king, we have been spared from the ravages of raiders from across the sea for a whole generation.'

Then Luke starts to sound gloomy. 'Things are now changing because of the traitor Sir Mordred and his heathen mercenaries, and there are rumours that those bloodthirsty Saxons are preparing to take advantage of the situation and attack us again. They've stayed away for the last twenty years, but these are uncertain and worrying days.'

He would make a good minstrel or songwriter as he has a way with words, even though he tells me he doesn't know how to read or write.

In the lower part of the hall are long refectory tables with benches along each side. Luke takes me to one of these, where a dozen boys are sitting; like him each of them works as a squire, a personal assistant to a knight. He tells me that one or two might become knights when they grow up, though suitability for admission depends more on noble birth than anything else.

Jasper is exhausted and lies by my feet.

Luke introduces me as Merlin's foreign guest. I'm unsure how I'm going to answer any questions, but to my relief the other boys don't pay much attention to me. They are obsessed with the rumours that Sir Mordred's army is threatening to besiege Camelot; this is the first occasion it's been endangered since King Arthur came to the throne. On the positive side they are looking forward to tonight's feast and to hearing the visiting troubadour perform his new ballad.

There's a roll of drums, and a trumpet fanfare sounds from an upper balcony.

Everyone stands to attention as a handsome, middle-aged couple walk into the hall.

The elegant lady is wearing a plain, ankle-length white dress buttoned up to her neck. On it is sewn a striking gold cross with four trumpet-shaped arms outlined by red stones and with a bright red ruby gleaming in the middle. The silver-haired man has a purple cloak, and both of them have plain gold crowns on their heads. They take their places at the Round Table next to Sir Perceval.

'There are King Arthur and Queen Guinevere,' whispers Luke.

I cannot believe that I am actually in the same room as the legendary King Arthur.

13 The Banquet

herald thumps the floor with a heavy staff and announces: 'Pray silence for grace.' Everyone stops talking while a friar in a brown cassock mumbles a long blessing in Latin. After a rousing chorus of 'Amen', the King and Queen sit and then the rest of the assembly take their places. People tuck in as soon as they can get their hands on any food – and they use their hands a lot. The cutlery is limited to daggers and wooden spoons, and doesn't include forks. There are just two meals a day here, at sunrise and sunset, so no one has eaten since breakfast.

All the ladies and girls of the Court are in an upper gallery, with the exception of the Queen, who is at the Round Table beside King Arthur.

'Why is the Queen the only lady sitting down here?'

'The Knights of the Round Table have declared her an honorary man as a special tribute,' Luke elaborates.

I don't reckon that most women from my century would consider that an honour!

At one side of the hall roasting spits are rotating over an open fire inside an enormous, walk-in fireplace. A couple of wild boar, some sheep and a deer are being cooked, as well as lots of smaller creatures. Luke licks his lips as he points out the geese, hares, badgers and hedgehogs, which are a great delicacy. A pair of swans has been sent over from Glastonbury's monastic swannery, but these are reserved for the King and his companions.

The poor cooks have to blow the fire with bellows, turn the spits around by hand and baste the meat with fat. They look exhausted and half-roasted themselves.

Everyone picks up food with their dirty fingers from the middle of the table and burps a lot; my mother would not be impressed by the table manners. Dogs are allowed in the hall, and bones and scraps are thrown to them, often causing much snarling and growling as they compete for food. I give a few choice pieces of meat to Jasper, who isn't used to fighting for his meals and has the good sense to keep out of sight under the table.

Even the young squires drink alcoholic mead or ale, decanted from enormous casks and served at the table in stone flagons or pottery jugs.

A cup of ale is poured for me. 'What's it made from and will it make me drunk?' I wonder.

'It's brewed with malted barley and is much safer to drink than water if you don't want to risk getting sick; we always drink ale. It's not very strong but has enough alcohol to stop it going off.'

I sip it and don't find the taste too unpleasant, but take care not to drink much. A can of cola would go down a storm here, even without any ice or refrigeration.

Luke tells me that this feast is an exception; the regular everyday food in Camelot is plain 'pottage', a stew made by boiling grains such as oats or barley into a porridge, with a few

vegetables or small amount of meat thrown in. It is flavoured with herbs, as salt is a great luxury. Pepper was imported to Britain from the Indies by the Romans but isn't available these days, so Luke is astounded to hear that salt, pepper and sugar are all common in my country.

There aren't any glasses, just earthenware cups without handles for most people. The Knights of the Round Table have more elaborate horn drinking vessels and metal spoons. The King and Queen use silver.

At the banquet, meat is served on square boards with a circular dip in the middle. Luke tells me: 'These platters are called "trenchers" and are carved out of stale bread. The meat juices soak into the trenchers, and after the feast they are distributed as alms to the poor.'

This certainly saves on washing up!

Following a trumpet fanfare a herald introduces the Celtic bard Taliesin of Caerleon, to great applause. A middle-aged man, who reminds me of an ageing hippie rock star, saunters into the hall strumming on a portable harp around thirty inches long with twenty-four strings. He is dressed in more colourful and flamboyant clothes than anyone else.

He doffs his feathered cap with a theatrical bow towards the King and Queen. The King acknowledges him, and then the minstrel entertains the company with ballads about chivalry and the exploits of the Knights of the Round Table. Everyone listens with great attention to his latest composition about Sir Gawain and the Green Knight; it tells the story of a great challenge that took place early in King Arthur's reign.

The repetitive melody is a bit tuneless and much slower than rap, but the words narrate a gripping, action-packed saga.

After the musical interlude the entertainment continues with the court jester, a stand-up comic who tells stories that are neither very funny nor much appreciated. He's known as 'The Fool', and is mocked cruelly. When he's tripped up near our table, Jasper goes and licks the man's face; this sympathetic gesture causes some laughter.

The lads at my table keep on repeating how this delicious feast is such a treat, but the tough meat and dense brown bread are unappetising and worse than school lunches.

I taste Luke's favourite, roast hedgehog, but find it unpleasantly fatty. There's no vegetarian option and no rice, potatoes or pasta. There isn't even any salad, though a few vegetables are served: broad beans stewed in meat fat, over-boiled cabbage, leeks and carrots, which aren't orange but range in colour from dirty white to purple.

I cut a slice of mutton and some bread to make a sandwich.

'How clever!' Luke comments. 'Is that how you serve meat in your country?'

'Sometimes. It was thought up by a lord, the Earl of Sandwich, so he could eat without having to get up from the gambling tables.'

'It would be handy when on the march,' comments Luke. 'I'll suggest it to the quartermaster. We could name it a "henry" after you if the idea catches on. We couldn't call it a "sandwich" as that sounds far too silly, and people would make stupid jokes about it.'

I agree that a 'henry' sounds far more distinguished.

Carried away by this success I consider telling him about hamburgers, but remember that potatoes and tomatoes weren't introduced to Europe from America until the sixteenth century.

Camelot is not ready for such civilised delicacies, and it is only right and proper that the burger should wait another thousand years until it can be served with ketchup and French fries.

I am staggered to find that the boys at my table are at least thirteen years old, as they are all shorter than me. The adults aren't tall either, and few of the Knights of the Round Table are much more than five feet eight inches.

The desserts are very plain and limited to boiled savoury puddings served with berries, and round pastries baked in honey called 'crispels', which are popular with the boys. The lack of sugar in Camelot doesn't bother me, but the complete absence of chocolate is a serious hardship.

Most people are slimmer than twenty-first century Britons, so the Camelot diet might have some health benefits. They drink lots of ale here too, which supports Dad's argument that a pint or two of beer is good for you and doesn't make you fat.

There's a packet of lemon sherbet sweets in my pocket, left over from my birthday party. I offer them round the table, and the boys' eyes almost pop out of their heads. None has ever tasted sugar, let alone fizzy sweets. Most are flabbergasted and keep taking them out of their mouths and examining them.

A red-haired lad says he's never tasted anything so thrilling, and keeps repeating: 'My mouth is alive.'

'This might be witchcraft,' suggests Lambert opposite, staring at me across the table in an ominous way and clenching his fist. Luke whispers that this is a gesture of defence against sorcery.

I start to panic, remembering what Merlin has told me about how suspected witches are tested by ordeal. Losing my cool, I hurry to reassure them that the ingredients are one hundred percent natural and organic, with no artificial additives or preservatives.

None of the boys understands a word of this, but my alternative explanation, that the sweets are made from dried fruits and plants from across the sea, seems to set their minds at rest.

I'm starting to build up my self-confidence. I am bigger than other boys of my own age, and also know much more about all sorts of things.

Perhaps Merlin was right: I am like a learned magician compared with these simple folk. But how might my knowledge of the future help me get back to my own century?

14 The King

The King spends most of the meal in earnest conversation with Sir Perceval. When they finish eating, he beckons to a man at arms and points him in our direction.

The soldier comes straight over to me: 'Are you the visitor, Henry?' I nod.

'Please come with me. His Majesty commands your attendance.'

Luke wishes me good luck. 'It's a great honour to be presented to the King when he's seated at the Round Table. You must be very important to have audiences with both him and Lord Merlin on your first day in Camelot.'

I tell Jasper to stay under the table and leave him chewing contentedly on a huge bone. Luke agrees to look after him and my rucksack, and I stand up with butterflies in my stomach. I've never met a king before!

We stop near the Round Table, and two more armed men come and stand to attention beside us.

Then King Arthur turns and beckons me to approach. He appears strong and dignified as well as gentle and kind; his eyes smile while the rest of his face shows little emotion. His aura of majesty is obvious, and I see why he commands such loyalty and devotion.

'Welcome to our Court, Master Henry. Lord Merlin tells me you come from a far-off land and possess great learning about arcane mysteries and occult devices. Are you prepared to use your knowledge and risk your life in a perilous quest to uphold righteousness and help us defeat the forces of evil?'

'Yes Sir, Your Majesty.'

I speak without pausing for thought and with no idea what I am letting myself in for, but can't turn down this renowned hero. According to Merlin there's no real choice, as this offers me my best or only chance to return home.

'I thank you and will be forever in your debt,' says the King. 'You should prepare to leave tonight after the banquet. I understand you already know Sir Perceval, who will accompany you for part of the way and will instruct you on the precise details. Your task is of the utmost importance to the future of civilisation.

'The core of the dilemma confronting us is that many years ago my evil half-sister, the sorceress Morgana Le Fay,

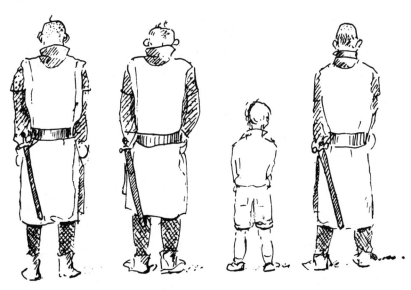

stole the enchanted scabbard of my sword Excalibur. The scabbard that held the sword is even more powerful than the blade, because its magic force protects its holder from all injury and makes him invulnerable. It also teaches us how a weapon can be strongest when sheathed.

'We all assumed it was lost forever, but Morgana hid it and was waiting for an opportunity to use it against us. Now it has reappeared in the hands of her son, the renegade knight and foul traitor Sir Mordred. Ruffians, cutthroats and opportunists without any loyalty believe he can't be defeated while he possesses the scabbard, and are flocking to support his rebellion. He is intent on destroying Camelot and all it stands for, bringing an end to our culture of honour, chivalry and romance.'

'That's terrible. How can I help, Your Majesty?'

'Merlin consulted the runes and foresaw that you are the one person who might get the scabbard away from Sir Mordred. Therefore I have decreed that you should be sent on this vital mission,' King Arthur states.

'Your task is to recover my scabbard from the traitor, for Sir Perceval to bring back here. If that isn't possible, then it will suffice if you can hide it. Once Sir Mordred's men think he has lost the scabbard and is no longer invincible, many will desert and he will have to end his rebellion and sue for peace.

'The survival of Camelot depends on your success. We have already sent some of our truest and best knights to try to recover the scabbard, but I regret they all perished in the attempt.

'Merlin advises that you possess unique knowledge and magical devices, and might be able to help, even though you are a mere lad. This is our last chance to avert disaster and prevent a dark age from overwhelming the realm. The minstrel Taliesin has agreed to accompany you to Mordred's camp, and you will be passed off as his assistant. You are to leave here tonight under cover of darkness.'

An awkward silence follows, while I digest the fact that I am expected to do better than any of the illustrious Knights of the Round Table, as some of their best have already failed and been killed trying.

Then the Queen turns towards me: 'How do you like our Court, young man?'

'It is very splendid and magnificent, Ma'am.' I try to talk in the sort of way you are supposed to address a queen.

'Even compared with castles and palaces across the sea?'

'Yes, Your Majesty.'

The Queen looks reassured. 'Camelot is designed in the latest fashion, and much of our castle is built of stone. Merlin has devised something he calls "a chimney", which enables us to burn a fire and cook indoors without filling our hall with smoke.'

'That's a marvel,' I reply tongue in cheek. 'Whatever will they think of next?'

'There can't be many things still to be invented that could make life more comfortable,' Queen Guinevere announces with the certainty that often goes with ignorance. Little does she know that my ordinary home, with its electric lights, fitted kitchen, hot and cold running water and television, is far more luxurious than the most palatial part of Camelot.

The King and Queen both smile graciously and turn away, signalling that my audience is at an end.

15 The Quest

A red-faced knight stands up and bangs a heavy flagon of ale on the Round Table with a resounding crash. By Camelot standards he is overweight, and he's a bit unsteady on his feet, as if the worse for drink. He must be one of the knights Luke referred to earlier, who are too fond of the herbal liqueur prepared by the Glastonbury monks.

'Excuse me, Your Majesty,' he shouts in a slurred voice, 'but did I overhear that this lad is being sent on a perilous quest?'

'Sit down, Sir Boor, and carry on drinking,' taunts a fair-haired knight.

'Not that oaf again,' mutters another.

'I have a right to be heard,' insists the knight, leaning against the back of his chair to steady himself.

'Very well, Sir Boor, you may speak your mind,' the King declares.

'I demand to know if the young stranger is being sent on a perilous quest. If so then I invoke Article V of the Fellowship of the Round Table,' Sir Boor announces with a self-satisfied smirk.

A murmuring goes round the Hall: 'Sir Boor is invoking Article V.'

I turn to Sir Perceval: 'What is Article V?'

'It's one of the articles of association of the Fellowship of the Round Table. It's a rule that says we can't offer the great honour of a perilous quest to an outsider, if one of our own knights has never been on one and demands to go instead. Sir Boor is the "provisions knight", in charge of organising our supplies of food and drink, but he's never been sent on any important missions.'

I'm relieved by this intervention; I've no wish to be a hero and am happy to forego the prospect of getting hurt or killed.

The King whispers to Sir Perceval and then proclaims with a tone of authority: 'Sir Boor speaks the truth. We cannot offer the envied privilege of undertaking so challenging an exploit to a visitor, who owes us no allegiance. We are bound by our own rules to award the opportunity first to a Knight of the Round Table, and Sir Boor is therefore entitled to claim the right.'

'There you are,' says Sir Boor to the others in a cocky manner. 'This time you have to let me go.'

I don't let on how pleased I am to have been let off the hook. Getting killed is a privilege that should be reserved for adults and soldiers.

Knights mutter scathing comments to one another around the Round Table.

'Sir Boor is bound to mess things up.'

'You can't send Sir Boor. He's been taking too much medicine for his old war wounds and he'll only fall off his horse again.'

'He'll forget where he is or get lost. Often he can't even find his way to his lady's chamber.'

'He won't want to go in the morning when he's sober.'

'Silence!' orders the King. 'Sir Boor is a noble Knight of the Round Table and therefore takes precedence over any outsider.

However, we must also consider that Merlin has emphasised the necessity of sending Master Henry on this task, as predicted by the runes.'

'You mustn't ignore the runes,' says Sir Bedivere, a serious knight sitting near Sir Perceval.

'That's right,' agrees another, 'you disregard such omens at your peril.'

After a short pause King Arthur announces his decision: 'The only solution is for me to make Master Henry an honorary Knight of the Round Table, and then according to our regulations he will be entitled to undertake this expedition. Who will propose him?'

Sir Perceval promptly takes the hint: 'I will.'

'You can't make him a Knight of the Round Table,' complains Sir Boor. 'He's only a boy. Why can't I be sent on a glorious mission?'

At this point he lets out a loud belch, breaks wind and sits down with a sheepish look.

King Arthur decrees: 'There's no age limit set down for knighthood in our statutes, and I can dispense with any of the usual qualifications and tests, or trials of skill and bravery in an emergency such as this. Master Henry, do you hereby swear fealty and allegiance to me, and promise to uphold the Code of the Fellowship of the Round Table with honour for glory until death?'

'Yes, Your Majesty.'

'Say "I do", and speak up,' instructs Sir Perceval, nudging me in the ribs.

I muster my most forceful tone of voice: 'I do.'

'Very good,' says the King. 'Please kneel. I hereby invest you as Sir Henry, Knight of the Round Table.'

I kneel down on one knee, and then King Arthur raises his illustrious sword Excalibur, the legendary weapon with which he has killed hundreds of his enemies in battle, and dubs me three times on alternate shoulders with it. 'Arise, Sir Henry. From this day I will support you as my faithful comrade in arms.'

Everyone claps and cheers, to my extreme embarrassment, and I am given a seat at the Round Table next to Sir Perceval.

People keep congratulating me, and I am in a total daze. I have never felt so important in my whole life.

Then a knight from the far side of the table speaks out in a voice loud enough for all to hear.

'You're not missing out on much, Sir Boor. It's an impossible task, and young Sir Henry is unlikely to survive for more than a day or two. I bet he'll be the shortest knight of the year in every sense. Let's call Sir Henry "the Midsummer Knight", because that's the shortest night in the calendar.'

Even the King and Queen laugh at this clever pun, and Sir Boor cheers up. I don't like the sound of it, and wish Jasper and I had never come to this brutal place. It's a cruel nickname, referring to my short life expectancy and not my height.

I make a private resolution that if I manage to get home against the odds, then I'll always eat the food Mum cooks, whether I like it or not, I will try to improve my table manners and will even have a bath or shower every day without arguing.

But all the good intentions in the world don't make the slightest difference to my current predicament. It looks as though I can't go home without first embarking on a life-threatening expedition, where I might well be killed.

16 The Wagon

When the King and Queen withdraw from the banquet and retire to their private quarters, Sir Perceval and his squire Luke escort the minstrel Taliesin, Jasper and me out of the Great Hall to the armoury and stables. It would have been a breach of etiquette to leave before the King. Most of the knights and courtiers carry on feasting, drinking and merrymaking in the Great Hall.

Taliesin is a cheerful, friendly character, and I warm to him straight away. He has a covered wagon pulled by a mule, similar to a tinker's caravan; it contains musical instruments, clothes, battered cooking pots, a few provisions and his meagre belongings. A nanny goat is tied to the back and walks behind.

I lift Jasper up first and then climb onto the wagon, which is decorated with advertisements for 'Taliesin the Bard of Caerleon, entertainer, necromancer and minstrel to kings, princes and emperors throughout the world.'

Luke is envious of my great honour and good fortune.

'You are so lucky to be made a knight. I wish I could swap places with you.'

Silently I agree, wishing someone else was going on this dangerous quest.

Luke performs his duties as squire, and helps Sir Perceval put on his armour and mount his horse; then Luke and Elaine accompany us out through the rear entrance of the castle, known as the postern gate, and down the hill as far as the moat and outer gateway. When our wagon leaves the protection of Camelot, they wish us good luck and wave goodbye.

'Be careful and stay safe!' Elaine adds with a look of real concern.

Are we ever going to meet again? I have an uncanny feeling that our paths are destined to cross once more in another place and time.

It has long been my dream to visit Camelot, but I don't belong here. Now my main desire is the exact opposite: never, ever to come here again – for a return to Camelot would mean a failure to get back to the future, my family and my friends.

It's a cloudless night, and a full moon illuminates the empty land with a silvery, dreamlike glow. The absence of lights and pollution makes the stars shine brighter than I have ever seen. Taliesin holds the mule's reins and steers the wagon, while Sir Perceval rides alongside.

'We should take the old Roman roads for most of our journey, even though it is a much greater distance,' Taliesin proposes, 'as we'll be able to find our way by moonlight and won't be arriving from the direction of Camelot when we approach the enemy camp.'

Sir Perceval agrees: 'I wouldn't want to take a mule wagon through the enchanted forest even in daylight, and certainly not at night.'

We head northwest out of Camelot on the track towards Glastonbury. After a couple of miles we come to a straight road with a hard gravel surface, wide enough for two carts to pass and with drainage ditches on both sides. 'This is the Fosse Way, a Roman road that crosses the land from Lindum to Isca,' explains Taliesin. 'Most of it is still in good condition, though it hasn't been repaired for over a hundred years since the legions left.'

My class did a project about this two-thousand-year-old highway, running for over two hundred miles from Lincoln to Exeter and linking the Roman towns that became Leicester, Cirencester and Bath. It passes a few miles northwest of my home in Sherborne.

We turn left onto this proper road, going southwest according to my compass, and travel at a walking pace. Sir Perceval joins Taliesin on the front seat of the wagon, ties his horse's reins to the back and starts chatting. 'Have you visited many distant lands?'

'Oh yes,' brags Taliesin. 'I've been all the way to the end of the earth. I once fell over the edge, but a friendly dragon rescued me.'

Sir Perceval is most impressed, and I don't interrupt or let on that our planet is round and that dragons don't exist. After today's events nothing I have ever been taught seems certain any longer, so I can't rule out that this alternative world might indeed be flat and inhabited by flying dragons.

The bleak countryside is desolate and deserted, and we don't see any other travellers or houses. Taliesin keeps up a continuous repertoire of songs and far-fetched stories, interrupted only by the occasional hoot of an owl or the shrill bark of a fox.

After a couple of hours we turn left onto another road at a junction near some ruins.

'In Roman days there was a prosperous walled town here called Lindinis, but it's derelict and abandoned,' Sir Perceval announces. 'We will now head south for two leagues, and then leave the road and follow the river Gifl upstream east to Camlann.'

These names are reassuring, as I learnt at school that Lindinis is the town we call Ilchester, and that Gifl was the old Celtic name for the river Yeo.

I lie down in the back of the wagon on a straw mattress and shut my eyes. Both Jasper and I are exhausted and soon fast asleep, oblivious to the lack of suspension and the hard, bumpy ride on solid wooden wheels without tyres.

Out for the count, I sleep for several hours, until Jasper wakes me with a lick to announce morning.

I forget where I am, and assume I'm having a weird dream. In my confused state I can't get my head around why I'm not at home in my bed. Then the amazing course of events since opening Merlin's summons comes flooding back.

I gaze up at my companions in disbelief. They aren't figments of my imagination but real flesh and blood. This is no dream.

'Good morning, I trust you slept well, Sir Henry,' says Sir Perceval. 'We are now arriving at Camlann, the place where I first met you yesterday.'

It's nice to be called Sir Henry and acknowledged as a fellow Knight of the Round Table, but these well-intentioned words upset me. Here is where my home ought to be – and yet it doesn't exist. Most distressing of all is the paradox that my parents haven't even been born. And yet I am now eleven years old, and King Arthur has declared me his 'comrade in arms', so I grit my teeth, determined to be brave and not to cry.

We enter the familiar woodcutter's hut, and I am relieved to see the magic stone, the only object that I recognise as existing both in the era of Camelot and in the twenty-first century. It is my link with the future, where Merlin predicts that the portal in time will open again at noon for Jasper and me to pass through and return to civilisation.

Sir Perceval notices me staring at it. 'This is the stone from which King Arthur pulled out a sword to be identified as our trueborn king. Afterwards it was hidden here by Lord Merlin.'

I acknowledge his words with a meaningful nod, already knowing about the stone and its magic.

Taliesin uses a tinderbox and dry twigs to light a fire, and boils up some oatmeal gruel: thin unsweetened porridge, which he serves in a tin with milk from the nanny goat. The lumpy mush looks unappetising, and I'd give anything for a bowl of my normal breakfast cereals, but I'm famished and eat it thankfully.

When we finish our breakfast, Sir Perceval says goodbye. 'For your own safety I mustn't travel any further with you. This is where I will await your return. If you head east towards the rising sun you should come across Sir Mordred's army before long. Good luck, Sir Henry. Try to find a way to lure Sir Mordred back here, so I can challenge him to a single combat.'

I don't know how he and Merlin expect me to achieve this, and I wish I could simply stay here with Sir Perceval until it's time to work the magic that might send me home. However, Merlin said his spell would only work if I'm brave and succeed in my mission for King Arthur, so I have no real choice but to carry on and face a fiendish enemy.

I therefore wave goodbye to Sir Perceval with regret, as Taliesin and I resume our relentless progress towards unimaginable dangers.

17 The Capture

Our mule-drawn wagon heads up a valley beside a small river, and I attempt to memorise the route between rolling, wooded hills. There are no roads or signposts, and to Taliesin's mystification I take compass bearings of any landmarks. I may need to navigate my way back here again in a few hours to activate Merlin's going-home spell at noon.

We have been travelling for almost an hour when ten fierce, bearded horsemen emerge from behind a clump of trees and surround us. They are armed with a hotchpotch of bows, spears and axes.

These hostile marauders search the wagon for loot, pointing their weapons at us with menacing gestures. When they find the musical instruments, Taliesin picks up his harp and starts playing and singing as if he hasn't a care in the world. This has a soothing effect on the ruffians, who confer among themselves and order us to follow them in the wagon.

'Where are you taking us?'

'You will find out soon enough,' says a swarthy, scar-faced man with a red beard, who's brandishing a sword and seems to be the leader of our abductors.

Then disaster strikes. One of the riders, who has a black patch over one eye, catches sight of my rucksack. It contains my precious birthday presents and also the magic cake and candle, the essential ingredients for Merlin's going-home spell.

Jasper tries to guard it, but the man snatches away the prize and hangs it onto a pommel of his horse's saddle. He fumbles with the zip but luckily he can't work out how to open it – if he finds and eats my magic cake, I'll never be able to get back to the future.

To my relief, someone mentions we are approaching Sir Mordred's camp. This is our intended destination, although we haven't planned on arriving as prisoners.

Taliesin warns me not to offend our captors. 'Don't say or do anything to annoy them or make them angry. They are wild barbarians from one of the minor Germanic tribes, maybe Jutes or Frisians, and are even more vicious than the ghastly Saxons. They hate Christians and aren't civilised like Celts and Romans, so they would slaughter us for idle pleasure; human life is not sacred to such savages.'

'Why are they fighting on Sir Mordred's side?'

'They support him because they think he's going to win, and he has promised them plenty of plunder and booty before the winter sets in. However, they have no loyalty and would change sides tomorrow if offered more gold and silver or easier pillaging.'

I doubt whether they can be quite that dreadful until I hear one of our captors say: 'If they are King Arthur's spies, Sir Mordred might let us use them for target practice later, like the last lot. Which of them do you reckon will run fastest? My money is on the little one.'

'I wager a silver piece that I can kill him with one arrow at fifty paces,' states his companion.

'Done!' They strike a deal, smacking each other's hands. They seem dead serious and don't appear to be fooling.

One of them stares at Jasper and starts licking his lips: 'How good would that odd creature taste in my stew? I bet its meat is delicious.'

I'm utterly sickened, and give my faithful companion a protective cuddle. It's a relief he doesn't understand what they are suggesting, but the situation is fast going from bad to worse.

This enemy camp has an atmosphere of menace and evil totally unlike Camelot.

Nobody looks kind or friendly, and most of these grim men are preparing for battle. Archers are making arrows or restringing their bows, some soldiers are repairing chain mail or hammering their shields into shape, and others are busy sharpening weapons on grindstones with an appalling grating noise.

Thousands of men are encamped in foul conditions of crowded squalor with none of the most basic facilities. There is no evidence of women, children, music, laughter, singing or even smiling.

Few of these grisly warriors have swords, shields or armour, and none of them wear uniforms. Most carry axes, or have longbows over their shoulders and a quiver of arrows on their backs. Their main protective clothing consists of leather jerkins or animal skins, though some have metal helmets.

In the middle of the encampment is a large, shabby brown tent, with a canopy and banners in front and a black flag. I shudder when I see two pikes stuck in the ground with bloody severed heads on top. A nearby tree is serving as a gallows, and there's a dead body blowing in the breeze. I have never seen a human corpse or smelt this stench of death before. It is horrible.

Opposite there's an enormous, hollow effigy of a reclining giant about twenty feet long, made of wicker basketwork. Imprisoned inside this weird cage are five miserable, half-naked wretches, pleading for mercy while laughing jailors poke them with sticks.

One of these tormentors notices my disgust and taunts: 'Want to get to know our wicker man, do you? That's where you might end up if Sir Mordred's in a bad mood or doesn't like the look of you. The wicker man is an ancient Druid tradition from the good old days before the Romans came, and at sunrise on midsummer's morning it will be set on fire with all the prisoners inside.

'The sight and sound of enemies being burnt alive is our favourite form of entertainment. It's a real fun spectacle that we all look forward to.'

I thought the Druids merely welcomed the midsummer solstice with solemn chanting, not in such a bloodthirsty manner, and I cross my fingers and pray I won't still be here to be at the centre of this horrific ceremony in a few days.

18 The Scabbard

A rmed guards in chain-mail armour prevent us from
advancing further.

The leader of the horsemen calls out: 'Tell Sir
Mordred we've captured some of King Arthur's spies. Shall we
put them to the torture now, or will he question them first?'

'We are not spies and we can be of great service to your
leader,' shouts Taliesin with a hint of desperation.

'Shut up,' orders our captor, thrusting his spear inches
from Taliesin's throat, 'or your next word will be your last.'

Then a sinister young man dressed in black strides out
of the tent and eyes us up and down with an expression of
contempt. He is sallow-faced, and unlike most of the soldiers
he has short, dark hair and is clean-shaven. A ferocious falcon
is perched on a thick leather gauntlet on his wrist, and he
is feeding it the bleeding innards of a baby rabbit. Even the
intrepid Jasper looks petrified.

After a worrying silence the man in black instructs the
guards: 'Bring the captives inside for interrogation.'

While climbing down from the wagon I pluck up all my
courage and snatch my rucksack back.

'Wait till I get my hands on you — I'll ensure you regret
this.' It doesn't sound like an idle threat.

Taliesin yells a warning as the angry soldier lunges at me and tries to seize the rucksack again. I am on the one-eyed man's blind side and turn just in time to catch his outstretched arm. With my best judo throw ever, a sneaky forward foot sweep that is almost a textbook *de-ashi-harai*, I use my assailant's momentum to trip him and leave him sprawling on his back in the mud. Judo techniques are unknown here, so the soldiers are astonished by my apparent strength, and ridicule their fallen comrade.

If only my friend Justin and our judo instructor could have witnessed my moment of glory!

I am now treated with more respect by the guards, who lead us into the tent. My humiliated would-be assailant grimaces with uncontrollable rage, gives me a penetrating glare and draws his hand slowly across his throat with a deliberate gesture of intent. He's a dangerous enemy who now bears me a very personal grudge.

Inside the tent, an ornately carved, gilded chair is raised up on a platform as a throne. Beside it is a chest with handles at each end, on which are laid out parchment manuscripts and crude maps. A black suit of armour and a gleaming assortment of vicious weapons are displayed on a stand.

Sir Mordred is seated on the makeshift throne, flanked on both sides by grim-faced bodyguards. To Jasper's relief the scary falcon is now hooded and motionless on a perch.

On a purple cushion at Sir Mordred's feet is an empty scabbard, partly covered with gold and encrusted with sparkling jewels.

I can't stop staring – it appears so precious and spectacular. Burning torches are fixed to the central tent post, and the reflection of their flames makes the jewels glint and glitter, as if they too are alight. I don't need to be told that this must be the objective of my quest: the magical scabbard of King Arthur's sword Excalibur.

Sir Mordred starts to interrogate Taliesin. 'Who are you and where have you come from?'

'Sire, I am Taliesin the Bard of Caerleon and this is my apprentice, Henry. I am a wandering minstrel and we have recently voyaged across the sea from Frankish Gaul, where I had the honour to perform for King Childebert of Paris.'

'Where are you now headed?' Sir Mordred asks him in an abrupt tone.

'We are on our way to play our music at next week's midsummer solstice festivities at the great stone circle of Stonehenge. I have entertained many kings throughout the world, even the Roman Emperor Justinian in Constantinople, and crave the great privilege of serenading you too, Sire.'

Taliesin's voice drops in a furtive, conspiratorial way. 'Furthermore Sire, our occult powers might be of service to you.'

Sir Mordred shows interest in this offer and all the name-dropping. 'I will hear your music. You may compose a tribute to me.'

Taliesin picks up his small harp and starts improvising a longwinded ballad, describing acts of great courage and bloodthirsty battles. The glorious name of Mordred keeps recurring, rhyming with red, dead, dread, head, bled and so on.

Sir Mordred smiles whenever he hears his own name mentioned with a complimentary or grisly connection. The more ridiculous and extreme the flattery, the more it seems to please him. If he does possess any good qualities, modesty certainly isn't one of them.

At last Sir Mordred has heard enough flowery praises about his valiant deeds, wisdom, strength, cunning and cleverness. He claps his hands to command silence.

'Your ballad has a simple, honest charm; but what sorcery can you perform to help me overcome my enemies? I don't need your assistance, though, as the magic scabbard of Excalibur already makes me invulnerable.'

He smiles and gazes with a smug expression at the precious scabbard on the cushion at his feet.

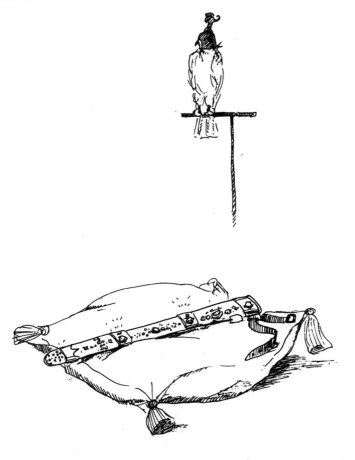

Taliesin glances from side to side, as if revealing important, confidential information. 'The powers that you seek are possessed by my young companion, whose arts of divination are far greater than my own, despite his tender years.'

Taliesin sounds as if he means it, but I don't know which way to turn. I have been dropped in at the deep end.

19 The Weapon

My pulse accelerates as Sir Mordred turns towards me with a disdainful sneer and an intimidating glare.

'Well? Speak now if you want your life to be spared. It had better be convincing, though, because I'm inclined to think you're both Arthur's spies, and the only good spy is a dead spy.'

He laughs at his own mediocre joke in an insincere way, and his attendants take the cue and join in, pretending to be overcome with mirth and hilarity.

With a miraculous stroke of luck a brainwave comes to me at just the right moment, and I try to appear confident. 'First, Sire, look at this.'

I open my rucksack, take out my telescope and extend it to its full length with a theatrical gesture. 'Please view through this tube, Sire.'

I hand the telescope to Sir Mordred and help him gaze through it from the wrong end. He is gobsmacked that everything appears so small.

'This is a marvel, but what practical uses does it have?'

'I have a magical weapon hidden near here, which can shrink your enemies and their weapons to a fraction of their size. This tube shows you how that might be.'

Sir Mordred is impressed, and passes the telescope to one of his henchmen, who looks through it and appears flabbergasted.

'You must bring me your device, and if it works I will spare both your lives and reward you with fifty Aurei gold coins. On second thoughts, take me to it in person this instant.'

My plan is succeeding, but I don't want to appear too keen.

'Can we trust you not to harm us? How can we be sure you won't break your bargain when you've got our weapon in your hands, or use it to make us smaller?'

'You have my oath. But one false move and you will die...' He pauses for dramatic effect before emphasising his next words: 'with extreme pain and suffering.'

I'm sure we can count on him not going anywhere without the scabbard, both to protect him from enemies and keep it safe. I make a counter-proposal: 'My device is worth far more than fifty, but give us a hundred and you have a deal.'

'You can't bargain with him,' whispers Taliesin in genuine alarm. 'They say he has killed people just for failing to show him enough respect.'

I've heard of gangsters behaving like that in my century, so perhaps little has changed.

'Seventy – and that's my final offer. You're lucky I'm in a generous mood today,' Sir Mordred announces.

'We agree, Sire,' Taliesin answers before I can get another word in.

Sir Mordred orders his servants to help him put on his armour and helmet. Then he picks up the precious scabbard, buckles it onto his belt and swaggers out of the tent.

He and his personal bodyguard of six horsemen accompany our wagon as it carries me, Taliesin and Jasper away from the hostile camp. We retrace our route back towards the wood-cutters' hut, where our friend Sir Perceval should be waiting.

I can tell that Sir Mordred's men fear him, but they don't appear devoted to him in the way those at Camelot are to King Arthur.

According to my watch there is only one hour left in which to return to the enchanted stone, light the candle of time, eat the magic cake and summon Merlin's magic power to take me back to the future.

I don't belong here, and now want nothing other than to go home, before Jasper and I are trapped in this grim past for eternity.

20 The Challenge

I t's a relief to have escaped the clutches of the ruffians who want to use me for target practice and cook Jasper in a stew, but we are still in grave danger.

What would my schoolfriends say if they could see me now with these improbable companions?

I am working on a plan to get the scabbard of Excalibur away from Sir Mordred. It depends on Sir Perceval, but might also enable me to go back home, as long as Merlin's spell works.

The cart trundles round a corner between thick curtains of trees, and we are again in the clearing where I first arrived in the era of Camelot yesterday. I cross my fingers in nervous anticipation; my life depends on Sir Perceval watching out for us from inside the hut.

'If you can get the scabbard away from Sir Mordred you must do so,' Taliesin whispers. 'Don't worry about Sir Perceval and me; we can take care of ourselves.'

Taliesin points out the hut to Sir Mordred. 'There is our destination.'

'Where is your magic weapon, boy? Take me to it at once,' Sir Mordred demands eagerly. 'But if there are any tricks, you are dead men walking.'

'Please follow me, Sire.'

Taliesin stays on the wagon, and Jasper runs ahead into the hut. I follow with Sir Mordred and three of his men.

To my relief Sir Perceval is waiting behind the door, sword in hand. As Sir Mordred crosses the threshold, he strikes him on the face with his gauntlet, an armoured glove, and then hurls it to the ground.

'Sir Mordred, you are a traitor and a coward. I hereby challenge you to a trial by combat according to the rules of chivalry.'

Sir Mordred, with the double protection of superior numbers and Excalibur's scabbard, picks up the gauntlet with a mocking laugh. 'I accept your challenge, you miserable wretch.'

Sir Perceval and I don't let on that we know each other, but Jasper goes up to him like an old friend and almost gives the game away. It's lucky that Sir Mordred doesn't notice.

'You need to be taught a lesson, young Perceval, unless you see sense and change sides. However, I'll give you one last chance to save your skin by paying homage to me instead. I can promise you that no one will even remember Arthur and his half-baked ideals of honour and courtliness in a few years, let alone the absurd spirit of Camelot nonsense and the ridiculous Round Table.'

I would love to be able to tell Sir Mordred how utterly wrong he is.

'Never,' responds Sir Perceval. 'I will fight to the death for my rightful liege lord, King Arthur Pendragon.'

I reach into my rucksack when nobody is watching, take out my bike siren and switch it on.

The piercing weeee-errrr sound of an ambulance, accompanied by blue flashes, makes both knights stop talking and stare at me in wide-eyed terror.

93

I point the gadget at Sir Mordred as if holding a gun. 'Here is the device you seek. Stand still or you will be shrunk to a quarter of your normal size. Even your scabbard won't protect you from its magic.'

Both knights freeze, uncertain what to do. Sir Mordred speaks with less forcefulness than before: 'What do you want?'

I recognise that, like most bullies, he's also a coward, the sort of creep who'd be a cyberbully in my world; so I try to sound convincing and hope my knees can't be seen shaking. 'While you two settle your argument outside, you must leave your scabbard inside the hut, or else it would not be fair. If you are victorious, I will hand over my weapon to you as we agreed.'

Sir Mordred accepts after a moment of hesitation, but says he must confer with his bodyguards first. He goes outside and gives his men some instructions.

Sir Perceval smiles and pats Jasper when we are alone: 'I think I can beat him in single combat.'

'If I manage to disappear during the fight, I'll try to bury the scabbard under the floor of the hut for you to recover later and take back to King Arthur. Good luck!'

Sir Mordred swaggers back in with three of his men and lays the precious scabbard of Excalibur on the stone table.

'Captain, if you value your life keep my scabbard, the young wizard and his magic weapon secure in here while I'm disposing of this troublesome knight.'

'I'll slit the lad's throat with my dagger if he tries anything, Sire,' says the first soldier with a malevolent leer.

It's clear that he not only means this threat, but will enjoy carrying it out.

As soon as Sir Mordred leaves the hut, the captain turns towards me. 'I don't fear your sorcery. I'm not superstitious like the boss, and I place all my trust only in cold steel. If you want to live a little longer don't move a single muscle.'

Jasper snarls at this sadistic thug, who doesn't take his eyes off me. Two more of Sir Mordred's men are stationed outside the door, and the other three are guarding Taliesin and his wagon at the far end of the clearing.

I need to be on my own soon, if I'm to have any hope of getting home again to my own century, my friends and my family.

But how on earth am I going to get rid of the murderous guard?

This dimwitted lout, who's staring at me like a hawk, is far too unimaginative to be fooled by any make-believe, pretend weapons.

My time is running out, and the situation is becoming desperate.

21 The Snake

Through the half-open door I watch as the two knights turn back-to-back, stride twenty paces and stick their swords into the ground. Then they mount their horses and charge at each other with wooden, steel-tipped lances.

On the first pass Sir Perceval's lance lands a magnificent blow on Sir Mordred's shield and almost unseats him, but he clings on. On the second pass Sir Mordred feints with great skill, dodges the lance and strikes Sir Perceval on the chest, knocking him off his horse. While Sir Perceval is still lying on the ground winded, Sir Mordred dismounts and runs at him with his mace, a spiked metal ball on a chain, swinging it with a menacing shout: 'Prepare to meet your maker, you miserable fool.'

Sir Perceval manages to roll over and avoid the vicious swipe from this lethal implement, and struggles to his feet with extraordinary agility for a man in full body armour. He is able to interpose his shield and block the second swing from Sir Mordred's deadly weapon, which is so violent that it dents his shield. Then, while fending off a succession of ferocious blows raining down on him, he staggers backwards towards his sword and grabs hold of it.

Sir Mordred drops the mace and runs to seize his own sword too. Now both knights are on their feet and once again on equal terms, smiting and defending with all their strength. Their heavy metal swords ring out like bells each time they clash. This conflict doesn't have much finesse; it is all about brute force, blood and guts. Both fighters are trying their utmost to kill or maim the other, with no holds barred and no rules of fair play.

I watch in amazement, having never observed anything half as violent. This duel with swords is nothing like an Olympic fencing bout, but is a genuine contest of life and death, a battle for survival. Sir Mordred seems to be getting the best of the cut and thrust, and I worry that Sir Perceval is being overpowered and beaten back by a stronger man.

Then I realise that he is deliberately trying to draw his opponent away from the scabbard and me.

When the combatants are at the other end of the clearing near Taliesin's wagon, I glance at my watch. To my horror it's coming up to midday.

Desperate to get the guard out of the way, I try to start up a conversation: 'Good fight isn't it? I bet you're skilled with a sword too.'

'Yes, but I prefer killing dogs and children with this.'

The thug thrusts his spear towards Jasper and smiles with a sadistic, lopsided grin as my intrepid little dog jumps out of the way and barks at him defiantly.

He turns his back for a second to observe the mortal combat outside, and I feel inside my rucksack, hoping he won't notice. My hand comes across my one unused birthday present: the battery-powered imitation snake. I doubt if it can help much, but give it a try.

In one brief movement I pull it out, flick on the switch and drop the wriggling snake at the guard's feet. Jasper draws his attention to it with a furious fit of barking.

To my relief the effect is little short of miraculous. This thick brute seems fearless, but he must have a phobia about snakes. He can't leave the hut fast enough, and in his hurry doesn't even take his spear.

He slams the door behind him, and I hear him tell his colleagues: 'There's a venomous serpent in the hut — it might do our job for us and kill the lad before we have to get

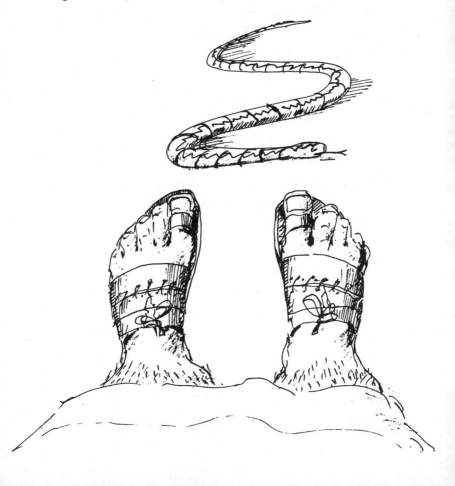

our hands dirty. There's no other exit, so he won't be going anywhere as long as we guard the door.'

This is alarming and sounds as though Mordred might have already told them to murder me after the combat.

I have got to get away from here!

I can still hear the clank of armour, the clashing of swords and the dull thuds of powerful blows parried by shields. Jasper and I are at last alone in the hut with both the precious scabbard and my rucksack. There's so much to do in just a couple of minutes.

I turn off the snake and start digging beside the base of King Arthur's stone near the hearth. The floor is bare earth, and the guard's sharp spear makes an effective spade.

I work at a feverish pace and manage to excavate a shallow trench, big enough to conceal the scabbard, which I wrap in the cloak Sir Perceval lent me.

I lay my precious load in this trench, cover it over with earth, sprinkle a handful of ash on top from the fire where we cooked our breakfast and stamp it flat to make it blend in with the rest of the floor. Without a proper search it might escape attention.

The swordfight continues outside – but the blows are landing with less frequency and force, as if both contestants are becoming more tactical and trying to test the other's weaknesses. Maybe they are also getting tired because their weapons are so heavy.

Then I hear one of the guards ask his companions: 'Should we get involved and help Sir Mordred finish off this fancy knight?'

'Not quite yet. Sir Mordred might even win without tricks or foul play this time; he told us not to interfere unless absolutely necessary, or when he signals.'

My watch indicates it is coming up to noon. Merlin's spell has to work for me this instant, or else Sir Mordred will find out that my 'magic weapon' is a scam and definitely bump me off, unless Sir Perceval defeats him and his cronies against all the odds.

Now is my one chance to pass through the portal in time, back to the future, to home and to civilisation.

22 The Return

I take the cake, candle and matches out of my rucksack, which also contains all my precious possessions from the future.

Then I hear one of the guards outside the door say: 'Weapons at the ready, men. There's Sir Mordred's signal for us to prepare to join in and attack Sir Perceval from behind. He's being driven towards us.'

I can't save myself and do nothing to help Sir Perceval and Taliesin recover the scabbard for King Arthur. I turn the snake on again and slip it under the door, hoping it will create a distraction and warn Sir Perceval about Sir Mordred's deceit.

Placing the cake on the stone I try to light the candle – but my hand is shaking so much that the first two matches break. On my lucky third attempt the candle flickers into life.

I put on my rucksack, pick Jasper up in my arms, take a bite of cake and give him a piece too. Then I walk three times clockwise around the stone, facing forwards as Merlin instructed.

Twice on each circuit I recite the rhyming spell, 'I summon Merlin's magic power to take me home this very hour.'

I have just completed the third and final circuit when a panicky voice outside says: 'May the gods protect us, there's that accursed serpent! We'd better check if it has already saved us the trouble of killing the boy.'

What will I do if Merlin's spell doesn't work and I am marooned in another world for the rest of my life? Unless Sir Perceval manages to defeat Sir Mordred, that might be very short indeed. I go all wobbly, and for a second it's as if a paralysing force is preventing me from activating the magic.

Too late I remember Merlin's instructions to leave nothing from the future behind. Still, I don't reckon that a toy snake can do much harm.

To my dismay the door of the hut starts to open. I manage to pull myself together, swallow my mouthful of cake, take a deep breath and blow out the candle. With increasing desperation I call out 'Merlin' seven times.

Dazzled by a brilliant flash, I feel the same spinning, dizzy sensation as at the start of my adventure, and again hear pulsating, accelerating noises.

I am almost too terrified to look, but when I open my eyes gingerly, it is as if a miracle has occurred. Jasper and I are back in my garden den, with the part-eaten cake and the candle on the stone in front of me.

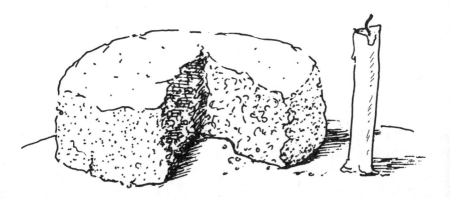

The woodcutter's hut has vanished, and the stone is half-buried under the ground and covered with moss, as I always knew it.

Then I hear the best and most wonderful sound in the whole world: my mother's voice. 'Henry – hurry up and come in at once. Didn't you hear me calling you for supper?'

I hug Jasper with a sense of total relief.

Could my amazing journey to the past have been imagined?

I wonder whether the powder I put in the cake might have been a drug after all.

I plod home exhausted and in a daze. Was my visit to Camelot a hallucination or daydream, or have I really spent nineteen hours in the era of King Arthur?

All my presents are still in my rucksack except for one: the battery-powered snake.

'How did you get so dirty; what have you been doing?' Mum scolds as I walk into the kitchen.

'Jasper and I have been to Camelot. I met Sir Perceval and Merlin, and King Arthur made me a Knight of the Round Table.'

'You look as though you've been rolling around in the mud. Go and wash your hands,' Mum tells me.

'Henry has such a vivid imagination,' I hear Dad mutter as I leave the room to clean up. 'You'd almost think he believes his fantasies are real.'

I eat my meal in silence, unsure what I can possibly say about my mind-blowing escapade.

'I'm whacked and would like to go up to my room. Please come and say goodnight later, Mum. Thanks for the lovely birthday tea and the presents. Love you!'

I even kiss my brothers in my relief at seeing them again. They are less than impressed by this uncharacteristic gesture.

Dad says: 'Sleep well and many happy returns of the day, Henry. Do you feel any different now you're eleven?'

'Yes – very different. Goodnight Dad. Thanks for everything.'

Coming home has literally given me the happiest return of my life, and today has changed me forever.

I undress, wash, brush my teeth and put on my pyjamas in a daze. Then I lie down on my bed to puzzle over the events of this extraordinary day.

Within minutes I am fast asleep.

23 The Treasure

I wake up later than usual on Sunday morning, but after breakfast can't wait to try out my new metal detector in the garden.

After an hour studying the instruction manual and experimenting with different sorts of metal, I master how to adjust its settings, sensitivity and volume. Then I set off with Jasper to my den, carrying the metal detector, my knife and a spade.

I dig down around King Arthur's stone, scouring the area for any trace of precious metal, but all I find is an old tin can.

Then Jasper starts scratching with his paws as if trying to show me where to search, so I investigate deeper at this precise spot. Can he smell something, or remember where we buried the scabbard yesterday or fifteen centuries ago?

I pick up a faint indication of metal and carry on, alternately digging and checking where the signal is strongest. There's a quiver of expectation as my spade touches a solid object that isn't stone, and Jasper's barking becomes more and more animated.

Brushing away the dirt I see a glint of gold. I work with my knife and my bare hands and uncover the scabbard of Excalibur where I hid it beside the stone, though now the ground level is more than a foot higher.

Much of the wood and leather parts of the scabbard have rotted away, any ordinary metal has turned green with age, but the gold and jewels are intact and untarnished. The cloak that had been around it has disintegrated.

I wrap the scabbard in my sweater and carry it back into the house in triumph, now knowing for certain that my journey to Camelot was real. I am holding the proof in my hands.

It distresses me to think that Sir Perceval can't have won the encounter with Sir Mordred. Otherwise why has the scabbard remained buried here for me to find and dig up again now?

I console myself with the realisation that this indicates a success in the main purpose of my mission for King Arthur, since it means that Sir Mordred can't have recovered the scabbard either.

I lay my cherished burden on the kitchen table before calling my family to come and see what I've found. I have mixed emotions, feeling thrilled but strangely sad too.

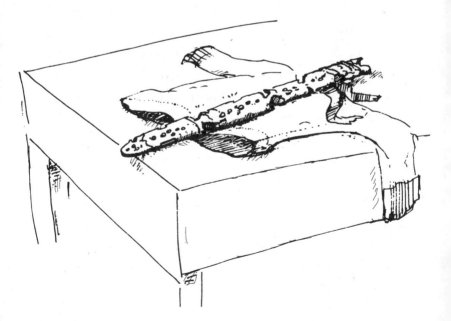

When my parents and brothers are standing round, I open up my sweater to reveal the scabbard.

There is a stunned silence before Dad speaks: 'It must be very old, and those might be precious jewels – it could be worth a fortune. That looks like real gold. What incredible luck to find such an extraordinary object straight away.'

'It's unbelievable!' Mum keeps repeating, lost for words for the first time in her life.

Jack stands gaping at it open-mouthed, and George whines: 'I want one of those things too! It's not fair if Henry has one and I don't.'

In the next few hours the situation is taken out of my hands. Our neighbour, Dr Blore, arrives in response to an excited telephone call from Dad, soon to be followed by leading members of the local historical society, the curator of the Dorset County Museum and later by several newspaper reporters and photographers.

I have to show each of them how and where the scabbard was located. There is no point trying to dissuade people from digging and metal detecting around the area of my den in search of the sword that belonged inside the scabbard or other artefacts. No one finds any interesting relics, but my den is ruined and seems to lose its mystery and power of enchantment for me.

When I suggest this is the magical lost scabbard of King Arthur's sword Excalibur, most people laugh in a conde-scending, superior sort of way that makes me very angry. The newspaper reporters recognise it makes a good story, but they aren't convinced.

I soon give up trying to tell the truth; nobody believes me, as Merlin foretold.

During the next few weeks all my spare time is spent researching on the internet or at the library. I read everything I can find about King Arthur and the Knights of the Round Table, and try to learn what happened to them all in the end.

According to most accounts King Arthur and Sir Mordred arranged a parley in front of their armies at a place called Camlann, with a view to agreeing a truce. Each was highly suspicious of the other and was accompanied by fourteen men. The remainder of their troops stood back on each side, ready for battle if the peace talks broke down.

To everyone's surprise the negotiations started well, despite the deep mutual mistrust, until one of the soldiers saw a snake slithering towards him. Without thinking, he drew his sword to kill it. At once the other men suspected treachery and drew their swords too. Then both armies charged.

The snake was reputed to be an adder, as was the imitation one I left behind contrary to Merlin's specific instructions.

In the ensuing battle King Arthur was mortally wounded, while Sir Mordred and most of the remaining Knights of the Round Table met their deaths. The Arthurian golden age of chivalry and romance ended forever, Camelot was utterly destroyed, and soon afterwards the Saxons invaded and overran most of England.

The few surviving Knights of the Round Table are said to have made their way to the Abbey of Glastonbury near the battlefield, where they became monks. One account mentions that after the Battle of Camlann the dying King Arthur was taken to Avalon by Sir Bedivere and a Celtic minstrel called Taliesin. Reading this name cheers me up a bit.

But could it have been my electronic snake that triggered the final battle?

Perhaps Merlin's dangerous attempt to meddle with time and change the course of history was by its nature doomed to fail; if so, then my toy snake could have been the instrument needed to restore things to how they were always destined to be.

I remember Merlin's promise of a reward beyond my wildest expectations. He must have known all along that the scabbard was going to remain buried where I hid it!

This leads me to suppose that he didn't plan my visit from the future to return the scabbard of Excalibur to King Arthur, but just wanted to get it away from Sir Mordred, so he'd have to enter into peace negotiations.

I wonder if Merlin's real aim was to ensure the survival not of King Arthur, the mortal man, but of his legacy: the spirit and ideals of Camelot, which are remembered and still a cause of inspiration even today.

Everybody I met there must have died many centuries ago, and I can't reach any firm conclusions. Was I to blame, or was it simply an odd coincidence that a snake, like the one I left behind, sparked off the final battle at a place called Camlann?

I will never know if my journey back through time changed anything at all.

It happened so very long ago, and historians are unable to agree whether King Arthur and the Knights of the Round Table even existed, let alone where or when.

Lost in the fog of history is the chronicle of the extraordinary adventure of young Sir Henry, who was a knight for a day.

24 The Reward

The following report appeared in *The Times* not long after these events:

GOLDEN DISCOVERY MAKES 11-YEAR-OLD A MILLIONAIRE

A schoolboy has discovered what might prove to be the most valuable single object yet found by a metal detector close to an ancient public footpath in Dorset. A golden scabbard, around 1500 years old and encrusted with precious jewels, was found by 11-year-old Henry Wolf near his home in Sherborne. He was using a metal detector given to him for his birthday, only the previous day.

A spokesman for the National Council for Metal Detecting commented, 'I've heard of beginners' luck, but this is ridiculous.'

The scabbard was found a few miles south of the Iron Age hill fort of Cadbury Castle in Somerset, which has traditionally been identified as the possible location of Camelot. There has therefore been fanciful speculation that this might even be the lost scabbard of King Arthur's sword Excalibur.

The scabbard is one of the most impressive artefacts ever found from the Romano-Celtic period in Britain, probably dating from the early 6th century AD. It must have belonged to a very important king or leader, from an age of which little is known and few remains exist, when the Christian Celts and descendants of the last Romans were trying to hold out in the southwest of Britain against the invasions of Saxons and other Germanic tribes. This is considered the most likely era for King Arthur to have reigned, if he ever existed.

The finder acted correctly in notifying the authorities within 14 days, and the coroner has declared the scabbard covered by the Treasure Act 1996 as an item of gold or silver more than 300 years old. It therefore becomes Crown property and will be offered to the British Museum, who must pay the finder a reward based upon its market value.

Experts say that in view of the intricate craftsmanship and ornate design, and the rarity of important artefacts from this sub-Roman period, its value should exceed the £2.3 million realised in 2010 by a Roman cavalry ceremonial helmet, the last single item of treasure of comparable significance found in Britain. Archaeologists have conducted an extensive search around the area of the find, but no sword or other related items have come to light.

I am pleased the scabbard will now belong to the Crown. King Arthur and Sir Perceval would have wanted it to be restored to the rightful monarch of Britain at last, and I suspect Merlin might have known all along that this would come to pass.

My parents decide to invest most of the reward money for me until I leave school, but I insist on buying a few special presents, including a new car for Mum. I also pay for a holiday to Disneyworld in Florida for the whole family and my five best friends, whose birthday gifts played such an important role in my adventure.

It's great to visit this 'magic kingdom'. It is far less exciting than Camelot, but the food is a lot tastier and it's very much cleaner and more comfortable. I enjoy being a millionaire and able to afford such luxuries.

I now see everything in a different way and am conscious of how the legacy of the past influences the present.

No one in the time of Camelot, or even a couple of centuries ago, could have imagined inventions that we now take for granted: electricity, air travel, television, smartphones and the internet, to name but a few. Yet the pace of scientific progress is still accelerating, and the world is expected to change as much during my lifetime as it has during that of my grandparents.

We are all travellers through time, each on our own personal journey towards an unknown future.

Acknowledgements

My son Henry felt unfairly treated as a child because he'd never had a book written about him. His brother Jack was the protagonist of my story *Jack and the Monster*, first published by Andersen Press in 1988 and later in many foreign editions. His other brother, George, was the eponymous subject of mum Louise Graham's childcare diary *George's First Year* (Peter Halban, 1992).

My own mother was in the same class at her first school in 1928 as the real Christopher Robin (Milne), and her bedtime readings from *Winnie the Pooh* inspired my love of fictional stories about real people. I therefore remedied this regrettable omission in Henry's life by writing for him the Arthurian adventure story that he himself devised and suggested, in which he and our dog Jasper were the central characters, transported back in time to Camelot.

The story interweaves time travel, magic, knights in armour, castles, perilous quests and buried treasure. The classic films *Back to the Future* and *The Wizard of Oz* influenced Henry's theme for the story, as did *Treasure Island*, the *Narnia* books and *Doctor Who*. Henry also wanted a readable, modern equivalent of Mark Twain's *A Connecticut Yankee in King Arthur's Court*.

Twenty years later I rediscovered the notebook with my original handwritten draft in a drawer, substantially rewrote it and had it illustrated by my friend, artist Lincoln Seligman.

Henry is now a successful businessman, co-founder with his brother George of acclaimed fashion business Wolf & Badger.

Special thanks to Robert Hastings for editorial and publishing help, Ken Leeder for the design of the cover and map, Dennis Friedman, Susan Grossman, Joel Green, Thomas Oakland, Roy Stedall-Humphryes and all the friends and relations who have given advice.

I owe a particular debt of gratitude to my wife Louise and our son Jack for their considerable help and encouragement. They have each spent many hours correcting and editing drafts, and providing valuable constructive criticism.

Richard Graham
London 2015

Step out of time –
Treasures of the Temple

A year after the extraordinary events described in *Knight for a Day* and the discovery of the golden scabbard of Excalibur, Henry and his family go to Istanbul on his twelfth birthday.

In the old Roman area of the city Henry gets separated from his family, falls down a mysterious hole and is trapped in an ancient, underground catacomb.

He is hungry and it's dark. He hasn't got a phone, but in his pocket there's a book of matches with the address of his hotel. Since his time-travel adventure in Camelot, Henry has always carried Merlin's candle of time and a piece of the magic cake as a lucky talisman. He lights the candle and attempts a 'get me out of here' enchantment, along similar lines to Merlin's spell that transported him to and from Camelot the previous year.

Henry can't believe it will work, but then he sees a glimmer of light and is no longer trapped. However, on emerging from the catacomb he finds that he hasn't simply escaped, but has once again travelled back through time to the sixth century. It is June 534 AD, exactly one year after his adventure in Camelot. In the Roman capital of Constantinople, the Emperor Justinian has been on the throne for seven years, and is constructing the biggest and most magnificent building the world has ever seen: the Church of the Holy Wisdom.

Almost the first people Henry bumps into in Constantinople are four familiar faces from Camelot: Sir Perceval, Taliesin the Minstrel, Luke and his sister Elaine. They managed to escape after the death of King Arthur and the destruction of Camelot, and have just arrived in Constantinople by sea after many adventures.

They don't seem at all surprised to see Henry, because Merlin had told them they might meet him again here, and Luke even carries an enigmatic message for Henry from Merlin.

The Emperor has awarded an official Roman military triumph to his victorious General Belisarius, who has just returned from his reconquest of North Africa from the Vandals. Prominently displayed among the spoils of war in the triumphal procession are the fabled treasures of the 2nd Temple of Jerusalem, which had been taken to Rome by Titus after the Temple's destruction in 70 AD and were seized by the Vandals in 455 AD.

Sir Perceval is on a quest to find the Holy Grail, and has had a vision that the Holy Grail is among these treasures. Merlin told him that the way to resurrect the spirit of the golden age of Camelot is by restoring the Holy Grail to Jerusalem. Henry discovers the hidden meaning of Merlin's message: the power of the Grail can also send him back to the future.

At Justinian's court, Henry and his companions meet Belisarius's scheming legal counsel, Procopius, who is involved in re-codifying the laws of the Empire. Procopius is reporting in secret to the power-hungry Empress Theodora, but is also plotting to discredit Belisarius and undermine the Emperor.

Henry learns that this jealous and treacherous man is an untrustworthy ally who will try to betray them. However, they go along with him and devise a cunning plan to play on the superstitions of the greedy Emperor and trick him into handing over the Grail and allowing them to take it back to Jerusalem.